The Mystery of Wreckers' Rock

KU-592-982

The Three Investigators in

The Three Investigators
in

The Mystery of
Wreckers' Rock

Text by William Arden
Based on characters created by Robert Arthur

ARMADA

The Mystery of Wreckers' Rock
was first published in Armada in 1988.

Armada is an imprint of the Children's Division,
part of the Collins Publishing Group,
8 Grafton Street, London W1X 3LA.

Printed in Great Britain by
William Collins Sons & Co. Ltd, Glasgow

Contents

A Word from Hector Sebastian

Welcome, mystery lovers! Once again it's time to catch up with the latest doings of the amazing Three Investigators. This time the tireless young detectives fall headlong into a case when they innocently photograph a family reunion. Reunions are usually jolly occasions, but this one turns out to be filled with mysterious threats – ghosts, howls in the night – and people who don't want their picture taken!

In case you've never met the Investigators before, let me fill you in. First there's Jupiter Jones, the overweight leader of the team. Jupe, as the others call him, is known for his remarkable brain power. Next is Pete Crenshaw, a tall boy and a fine athlete, but a little nervous around ghosts. Last but not least is Bob Andrews, a slight, studious boy with a quiet sense of humour and a knack for research.

The boys all live in Rocky Beach, California, a town on the Pacific Ocean not very far from Hollywood. The boys' Headquarters is in a trailer cleverly hidden from sight in The Jones Salvage Yard. That unique junkyard is owned by Jupiter's aunt and uncle, who are his guardians.

That's enough for now. Adventure awaits on Wreckers' Rock!

HECTOR SEBASTIAN

1

A Sea Battle

The outboard motorboat heaved on the long swells of the Pacific Ocean near a small island with an enormous rock jutting up at its western end.

"It looks like the Rock of Gibraltar," Bob Andrews said.

"Vaguely, Records," Jupiter Jones said, consideringly, "but a little smaller, don't you think?"

"Like about a thousand times," Pete Crenshaw put in. "I'd call it the Pebble of Gibraltar!"

The three members of the junior detective team of The Three Investigators were fishing out in the sea some ten miles south of Rocky Beach, California. Jupiter resembled a plump Day-Glo sausage in his fluorescent life jacket. The First Investigator, though an athlete of the mind, was far from being a physical athlete. That was more true of Pete, the tall, well-muscled Second Investigator. He looked like an ad for sporting goods in his life jacket. Bob, the Investigator in charge of Records and Research, was studying the water as if a hard stare could produce a fish.

The boys were casting light sinkers and live anchovies near the kelp beds where the calico bass lurked. So far, the bass had shown little interest in their efforts. There were only three medium-size fish swimming lazily in their pail.

"I told you it'd be better back off Genoa Reef," Pete complained, reeling in to change his bait. "What does your dad want us to photograph way out here anyway, Records?" Bob's father was a reporter for a Los Angeles afternoon newspaper.

"He wouldn't say," Bob said. He let the line out slowly, alert for the quick bite of the bass. "Just that on Tuesday we should fish way out here off Ragnarson Rock and take my camera with us. He'll pay us if we get good pictures, but he didn't say of what. Just laughed when I asked, said we'd know it when we saw it."

"The fee is what interests me," Jupiter said. "The Three Investigators' treasury is abysmally low. If we don't replenish our reserves soon, we may have to go to work for Aunt Mathilda."

"Oh, no," Pete groaned.

They all shuddered at the dismal prospect of working in The Jones Salvage Yard for Jupiter's Aunt Mathilda. The junior detective team was on summer holiday, and Jupiter's formidable aunt considered this her golden opportunity to get some extra work done around the yard. The boys concentrated on their efforts to lure the elusive calico bass out of the safety of the kelp. If they caught enough fish, they would earn the much-needed pocket money. But no more fish would cooperate. Pete yawned and scanned the blue water around them. His eyes widened.

"Fellows!" the Second Investigator cried, and pointed toward the mile-long island of Ragnarson Rock.

A long, low Viking ship was sailing around the east end. The afternoon sun reflected off the shields hanging along its sides. A fierce dragon's head with a gaping mouth full of carved teeth knifed the air as the ship swept ahead. Wild warriors in horned helmets, beards, and thick fur jackets brandished swords and battle-axes. Flags flew from the mast and the high stern post. The warriors shouted hoarse battle cries.

"*That*," Jupiter said, "is certainly 'it'!"

Bob had his camera out. "My dad says he'll buy all the pictures we can take."

The Viking ship swept closer. The boys saw that it was

really only a large outboard motorboat with the replica of a Viking ship built on top of it. There were only six or seven "warriors" on the ship, and most of the swords were painted wood, the beards fake. The men waved their wooden weapons and laughed as the "long ship" sailed on past the boys and into a small cove on the island.

"What is *that* all about?" Pete wondered.

"I don't know," Bob said, "but I got some good pictures of them."

"I think – " Jupiter began.

The stout First Investigator stopped with his mouth open. A second boat had come racing around the eastern end of the island.

"What's that one?" Pete gaped.

The second boat was long and low and looked half like a rowboat and half like a canoe. It was made of big planks with both ends higher than the middle, like a big flat-bottomed fishing boat pointed at both ends. The unusual boat was being paddled in unison by six whooping "Indians" in full headdresses, beards, and buckskins.

"It's a Chumash plank canoe!" Jupiter realized. "They were our local Indians. They had a big village up in Santa Barbara and traces have been found of their seagoing canoes. Apparently they went out to sea to fish and chase whales and seals. They were very peaceful, and some of them lived out here on the Channel Islands."

"You don't have to give us a history lesson, Jupe," Pete retorted. "I remember them from the Mystery of the Laughing Shadow." He was referring to an earlier case the boys had solved involving the local Chumash tribe. "I just didn't know they lived right here on Ragnarson Rock."

Jupiter shook his head. "They didn't, Second. They lived farther up the coast on the bigger islands."

"Never mind where they lived!" Bob cried. "Hold the boat steady so I can get some more shots."

The Records and Research man of The Three Investigators aimed his camera at the plank canoe and its war-whooping Indians, who were racing on, brandishing spears, towards the same cove where the Vikings had landed. They landed, too, and a mock battle began between the Vikings and the Indians for possession of Ragnarson Rock. Flags waved and weapons collided. Headdresses tossed and spears were flung against shields. Tucked in the belt of each Viking and Indian was a piece of coloured cloth – red for the Indians, white for the Vikings. The men grabbed at one another's "flags" and raced for the giant rock itself.

In the boat the three boys laughed and cheered, Pete and Bob siding with the Indians, and Jupiter urging on the Vikings. As the battle approached the great rock at the western end, Bob reloaded his camera.

"Let's get in closer, fellows! If we get the whole battle, it'll make a great human interest feature for my dad's paper, and he'll buy more photos."

"An excellent idea, Records," Jupiter agreed.

They started the motor, and Pete steered them into the mouth of the cove. Bob took picture after picture until the battle was over and the Vikings stood on top of the rock with all the red flags. They waved the captured red flags and their own white Viking banners. Everyone on the island was laughing now, congratulating one another.

In the boat, Bob stopped taking pictures. All the boys smiled at the hilarious scene on the island. Until Jupiter happened to glance over his shoulder.

"Second! Records!"

Another boat was about to hit them!

2

The Empty Boat

The small motorboat came right at them – then gently bumped them, bobbed on the small swells of the cove, and bumped their boat again.

"It's just drifting," Pete realized. "The motor's not even running."

"And there's no one in it!" Bob cried. "Look, the anchor rope's trailing in the water. It must have broken loose from somewhere."

Pete examined the ragged end of the rope. "It sure wasn't cut. It looks as if it just wore through when the anchor was down. Maybe rubbed against the rocks or a dock or something."

Jupiter had said nothing, his quick eyes examining the empty boat. Now the First Investigator suddenly pointed to the rail near the centre seat.

"Look, fellows. On the rowlock and near the seat!"

The other two Investigators examined the dark stain on the grey metal rowlock and on the edge of the boat – a dark red stain, almost black in the afternoon sunlight.

"I-it looks like . . ." Pete quavered.

"Blood!" Bob finished.

"Yes." Jupiter nodded. "As if someone cut himself, or" – the stocky leader of the team hesitated and looked at his companions – "or perhaps fell and hit his head on the rowlock."

Pete held the empty boat close to them. They all stared into it. There was a tackle box on the bottom near the centre seat, a bucket of water with dead anchovies floating thickly, an open lunch box that still contained some sandwiches and an apple, and a large life jacket like the boys had on.

"Everything," Jupiter said slowly, "except a fishing rod and reel."

"Jupe?" Bob said uneasily. "Under the seat. See? Is that a hat?"

Pete held the drifting boat with one hand and reached under its centre seat. He came up with a long-billed fisherman's cap. There was a tear in one side and more dark stains like those on the boat.

Jupiter's voice was serious. "Someone was hurt in this boat, fellows. The question is, where was the boat when it happened?"

"What do you mean, First?" Pete frowned. "What does it matter where the boat was?"

"Jupe means, was the boat out on the ocean or maybe tied up to shore?" Bob said. "That'd make a lot of difference."

"And was the fisherman alone in the boat?" Jupiter added. "I mean, did someone in another boat pull alongside, take him ashore, and get help, and the boat was left alone and drifted away? Or did the owner just . . . fall overboard?"

Pete and Bob glanced at each other in alarm.

"Or," Jupiter said, "was there someone else in this boat?"

Pete paled. "You think the fisherman w-was murdered?"

"Let's not jump to conclusions," Jupiter said carefully. "All we have here is circumstantial evidence."

The three boys sat silently for a moment, gazing into the empty boat with the dark stains. Bob finally spoke.

"Maybe the boat belongs to one of those Vikings or Indians on the island. Someone got cut or something."

"That's possible, Records," Jupiter agreed. "I suggest we find out."

With Bob and Jupiter holding the frayed anchor rope of the empty boat, Pete started their own motor and sailed in closer to the island. The Vikings and Indians were trooping down the giant rock towards the cove, still waving their battle flags and slapping each other on the back. Some of the jubilant combatants saw Bob and his camera. They shouted to the boys as their boat neared the shore of the cove where the Viking ship and Chumash canoe and some other boats were beached.

"Hey, take our pictures!"

"Come on ashore, we'll pose!"

"Take us Indians!"

"No, the Vikings! We won!"

"Come on and eat with us!"

The three boys laughed and shook their heads.

"Does this boat belong to any of you?" Jupiter called across the water.

"Not us!" a Viking shouted back.

"Come on, take some more pictures." an Indian urged.

To encourage Bob, some of the Vikings and Indians assumed ferocious poses, holding spears and axes to one another's throats.

Bob grinned and snapped more pictures of the activities on the island. Tents were being pitched in rows on a bluff above the cove's beach, and around a large fire some women and children were setting out food for a picnic. Bob shot more pictures, sweeping his camera lens across the whole treeless island.

"Hurry up," Pete demanded, "or we won't have time to catch enough fish to make any money."

"I'm almost finished with the roll," Bob said.

"I'm sorry, Pete, but I think we must take back the empty boat immediately," Jupiter said. "Something terrible could have happened to its owner."

"Maybe we could radio the police," Pete suggested.

15

"One of those boats moored on the island might have a radio."

"Good idea, Second," Jupiter exclaimed, and called to the warriors turned picnickers. "Excuse me, are those your boats?"

Heads nodded.

"Do any of you have a radio in your boat?"

"Sorry," an Indian called back.

"Mine is broken!" a Viking shouted.

Bob took his last picture. "No more film. What do we do, fish or go back to shore?"

"I guess we take the boat in," Pete said glumly.

"That's our first priority," Jupiter insisted. "Someone might be in desperate need of help."

They tied the broken anchor rope of the empty boat to their stern, and Pete turned them for home. They were far out, and Jupiter looked anxiously at his watch from time to time as Pete drove them up and over the long blue swells of the ocean. They searched for a boat with a radio, but they passed none. Bob cleaned the few bass they had caught.

"At least we caught enough for our own suppers," Bob said cheerfully.

The drag of the second boat slowed them down, and it was after four by the time they reached the Rocky Beach marina.

"Hey," Pete said from the stern, where he was steering. "Isn't that Chief Reynolds on the dock?"

Jupiter and Bob turned to look.

"And he's got some of his men with him!" Bob declared.

They could see the imposing figure of Rocky Beach's chief of police on the long public dock where most people tied up their boats. Three of his uniformed men and he were gathered around a slender woman in a fashionable green dress. Her red hair caught the late afternoon

16

sunlight, and she seemed distraught. She wiped her eyes and stared out to sea as the chief talked to her.

"Who's the woman?" Pete wondered.

"Gosh, I don't know her," Bob said, "but she's sure watching *us* closely!"

The woman had stopped scanning the water and was now focused on the three boys. Her blue eyes were wide.

"Not us, fellows," Jupiter stated. "It's the empty boat. I think she recognizes it."

"Hey, maybe she'll recognize the hat, too," Pete said.

As they neared the dock, Pete reached down and held up the torn and bloodstained fishing hat. The woman turned white as a ghost and fainted into Chief Reynolds' arms.

3

An Angry Viking

The police and the three boys gathered around the pale woman as Chief Reynolds propped her up on a bench on the dock.

"Give her some air, boys," the chief said. "Now tell me where you found that boat."

Pete and Bob quickly related the events at Ragnarson Rock. Chief Reynolds listened carefully, and as they finished, the woman opened her eyes and struggled to stand up.

"I have to go out there!" she cried.

The police restrained the distraught woman, and Chief Reynolds spoke quietly to calm her.

"We'll have a helicopter out there within twenty minutes, Mrs Manning. You sit back and try to relax now. There's nothing you can do that isn't being done."

The chief smiled, and Mrs Manning slumped back against the bench. Her blue eyes darted around at them all. Chief Reynolds turned to the boys.

"Mrs Manning's husband went out fishing late last night, boys, and told her he would be back in time for work at eight-thirty this morning. He often fished overnight. He had lights and a two-way radio, and never went far offshore. But this morning he didn't come home, and at noon Mrs Manning called us. We came here and found his car still locked and no sign of him. No one had seen the boat since it went out last night. Not until now."

He spoke calmly so as not to alarm Mrs Manning, but his expression was grim as he examined the empty boat now tied to the dock.

Mrs Manning blinked at the boys, confused. "What was

Bill doing way out there? He never went out so far alone. He couldn't swim – that's why he always took the life jacket."

"We don't know that he did go out that far, Mrs Manning," Chief Reynolds reassured her. "A strong current often runs offshore towards Ragnarson Rock. The boys found the boat drifting this afternoon. It could easily have drifted out there from the shore."

"Then," she went on, "where's Bill?"

There was a tense silence.

"That's what we have to find out, Mrs Manning," Chief Reynolds said firmly. "I'm sure there's a simple explanation. Perhaps he came ashore, and the boat broke away and drifted out to sea."

"Then," Mrs Manning said, "why hasn't he come home? Or at least picked up the car?"

"We'll find out," the chief said. "We've already contacted the Coast Guard to start a search, and all the police departments up and down the coast are looking for him. It's possible he'll turn up all by himself with some reasonable explanation."

"Possible? That's all?"

Mrs Manning looked wildly at the patrolmen, at the boys, at Chief Reynolds. Her face was white. For a moment the boys thought she was going to faint again. Then she slowly shook her head.

"It's possible he'll turn up safe, but it's not probable, is that what you mean?" Suddenly she stood up and took the torn fishing hat from Pete's hand. "It's his hat. And that's blood on it, isn't it?"

"It could be," the chief admitted. "Yes."

"And on the boat?" She looked down at the empty boat tied to the pier. "Blood on the gunwale and on the rowlock. His fishing tackle not put away. No rod or reel." She shook her head. "Something happened out there – I

19

know it. Something happened, and Bill is never coming back."

She began to cry, sank down again on the dock bench, and sobbed into her handkerchief as the boys and the police stood there awkwardly, unable to think of anything to say.

"There's always hope, Mrs Manning," Jupiter said quietly. "His . . . his life jacket is still in the boat. Since he couldn't swim, he would probably keep it on all the time while out on the water. So it's quite possible he did go ashore somewhere by choice, as the chief suggests."

"Sure," Pete put in. "I mean, he wouldn't wear anything as big and uncomfortable as that life jacket on shore."

"And he wouldn't want to leave his rod and reel," Bob said. "They might get stolen."

She smiled sadly and shook her head again. "I can see you're nice boys, but Bill hated to wear the life jacket when he fished. He said it was too confining. He kept it close to him, but he liked to fish freely and listen to his two-way radio. The radio would have been in a big pocket in his fishing jacket, and it's gone, too, isn't it?"

Pete swallowed. "Er, yes, ma'am, it is, but . . . but . . ." He stopped lamely.

Mrs Manning went on shaking her head. "No, Bill won't be coming back to me. Something happened. He fell and hit his head and was probably unconscious when he went overboard." She looked up at them all. "I always told him to keep his life jacket on when he was out there. He just wouldn't. Now he's gone."

There was another silence on the dock.

"I'm sorry, Mrs Manning," Chief Reynolds said. "I'll admit it doesn't look good, but there's always a chance."

"Perhaps," Jupiter suggested hopefully, "he was picked up by a boat that has no radio and hasn't come in yet."

"Or he got out on Ragnarson Rock!" Bob said.

Mrs Manning stood up, smoothing her dress. She smiled thinly. "Thank you, boys, and you too, Chief. I know you all mean well. But Bill would never have gone far enough out for any of that to happen. He fished no more than a mile offshore at the most. He always said he could probably float a mile in a life jacket. No, he won't be back. That boat was empty long before it drifted over to that island. I'll drive our car home, Chief Reynolds, and I'll wait for you to call and tell me you've found his body."

She walked slowly away towards the car parked near the boat-launching ramp. The chief motioned for some of his men to go with her. Then he turned to the boys.

"You did good work, boys, bringing the boat in."

"Is . . . is there much chance he's OK, Chief?" Pete asked.

"It looks like he hit his head and went overboard, Pete, just as she said. He was alone in that boat, it was night . . ." The chief shrugged and didn't finish. "But we'll search thoroughly. You saw nothing else out there that might tell us what happened to Mr Manning?"

"Nothing, Chief," Pete answered.

"All right, boys, let me know if you think of anything," the chief ended. The Three Investigators had cooperated with the Rocky Beach police on a number of other stubborn cases and Chief Reynolds respected their sharp eyes.

The three boys nodded as Chief Reynolds returned to his car. When the police and Mrs Manning had gone, they tied their boat up securely and headed for their bicycles, chained to the harbour bike rack.

"Hey! You kids!"

A small outboard motorboat glided up to the dock, with one of the fierce Vikings from Ragnarson Rock at the wheel. He waved eagerly to them.

"Hold on. I want to talk to you."

21

The Viking deftly steered his boat next to the launching ramp, tossed a rope around a piling, and jumped lightly ashore. He wasn't very tall, and his heavy Viking fur tunic made him look as wide as he was high. His legs below the knee were wrapped in cloth leggings and leather straps. He had a fake yellow beard and wore a horned helmet with a long nose guard that almost completely hid his face. Only his blue eyes were clearly visible as he walked up to the boys.

"Are you the guys who were so shutter-happy out on the Rock today?"

"Is there something wrong?" Bob asked warily.

Jupiter's voice was cool. "We have a perfect right to photograph a public spectacle."

"Hey, take it easy," the Viking said. "I just want to buy them. I'll buy all the shots you took."

"They're not even developed yet," Bob said. "Besides, my dad has first call on them for his newspaper."

"OK, I'll go with you while you develop them. I really only want a couple, but I want to pick just the right ones."

"I'm afraid Bob's father wants to see all the pictures," Jupiter said, "and those he buys will be exclusive. But we'll be glad to show you what Mr Andrews doesn't want."

"That's right," Bob agreed. "I'll be glad to sell you what you want tomorrow after my dad's taken his, Mr . . ."

"Sam Ragnarson," the Viking told him. "Look, I'll pay really well. Just give me first shot at them."

Bob hesitated – the Three Investigators really needed the money.

"I'm sorry, Mr Ragnarson," Bob said unhappily. "My dad's counting on taking the photos down to LA as soon as I develop them. Come back tomorrow."

Sam Ragnarson's blue eyes glared, and his voice was suddenly nasty as he advanced menacingly on the boys.

"I said I needed them *now*, and I mean now. If you three stupid kids won't listen to reason, I can use other . . ."

They backed away in alarm. There was the sound of tyres and then a voice called to them.

"Boys, I forgot to ask if you moved anything in the boat," Chief Reynolds called to them from his car window. He had pulled up nearby on the boardwalk.

"Only the hat, sir," Jupiter said, moving quickly towards the chief. He went on to list everything else they'd seen in the boat.

The chief nodded and started to drive away again, and the boys looked quickly around. Sam Ragnarson was nowhere in sight. Even his boat was gone. They hurried to their bikes.

"I guess he doesn't like cops," Pete said.

"I'll say!" added Bob. "He didn't even wait to get my name and address. Now he'll never get his pictures."

"I'll take the film back to Headquarters," Jupe offered. "You can come over and develop it first thing in the morning, Bob.

"Meanwhile," he added, "keep listening to your radios. Maybe they'll find out something about poor Mr Manning."

4

Followed!

Early next morning Bob hurried down to breakfast to tell his father about the pictures. The night before, Bob had arrived home to find his parents had already left for dinner and the theatre in Los Angeles. Bob had been too tired to wait up for them. His dad was reading the morning newspaper when Bob entered the kitchen. Mr Andrews looked up at his son.

"I see you boys had a sad experience yesterday."

Bob nodded. "Have they found Mr Manning yet?"

"I have no idea, Bob. This was printed last night."

Mrs Andrews turned on the radio. "The local news should be just about starting."

The announcer finished the national news, reported on a local fire, and then said, "*The Coast Guard is still searching for William Manning, a Rocky Beach car dealer, whose empty boat was found near Ragnarson Rock yesterday by three Rocky Beach boys: Robert Andrews, Peter Crenshaw, and Jonathan Jones.*"

"Oh no!" Bob cried. "They got Jupe's name wrong again!"

"*Manning's wife reported that he could not swim, and little hope is held for the survival of the fisherman.*"

"That poor woman," Mrs Andrews said sadly.

"A nasty accident," Mr Andrews agreed. "But don't you have something else to tell me, Bob?"

"I sure do, Dad!" And he eagerly related the events of the day before at Ragnarson Rock as he wolfed down his cereal.

Mr Andrews laughed. "That sounds just about as wild as we expected. We'll run a full-page feature tomorrow."

"What on earth for?" Mrs Andrews said, amazed. "They sound like nothing more than a band of crazy overage kids."

"What *is* so special about them?" Bob asked.

"They're a piece of California history," Mr Andrews explained. "Back in 1849, Knut Ragnarson came out here from Illinois with the Gold Rush. He was a bootmaker, and he made a lot more money selling boots to the miners than most of the miners ever did from mining gold. So the next year he took a ship from San Francisco to go back East and get his family. The ship had a cargo of gold as well as passengers. The second night out, the captain opened the sea cocks to sink the ship, took the gold, and set off in the longboat. Most of the passengers panicked and were lost, but Knut Ragnarson ripped off a hatch cover and paddled it to that little island. He found an abandoned Chumash canoe on the island and sailed it to shore. Ever since then the island has been called Ragnarson Rock. The Ragnarsons and friends get together every five years to stage a mock battle and 'reclaim' the island. They camp out there for a whole week. Karl Ragnarson – your school principal – told me all about it."

"Mr Karl?" exclaimed Bob. "Was he out there at the battle too?"

"I'm sure he was," said Mr Andrews, "though I think he leaves most of the high jinks to the younger men. He's more interested in the family history."

"Speaking of history," Mrs Andrews put in, "whatever happened to the stolen gold?"

"And how long did Knut Ragnarson stay on the island?" Bob wondered.

Mr Andrews held up his hands and laughed. "Whoa! That's all I know about it. We've got a reporter researching the details now. With Bob's pictures, it should make quite a feature for tomorrow."

Bob finished his milk. "Jupe's got the film. I'll go over and get it developed right now. We should – "

"Hold everything, young man," his mother said. "Have you perhaps forgotten it's window-washing morning at the Andrews'?"

"Mom!" Bob protested, "I've *got* to develop the pictures for Dad!"

"You know the rules, Robert," Mrs Andrews declared. "One morning a week this summer you help around the house. You chose Wednesdays yourself so it wouldn't be constantly breaking into your plans. We agreed there would be absolutely no exceptions or I'd be chasing you all summer and nothing would ever get done."

"Mom," Bob pleaded, "just today? I'll – "

"I'll take the film down to the office and have it developed there," his father said. "I'm working at home this morning. I won't leave for the office till noon. That should give you enough time to do the windows for your mother and still get the film to me."

Reluctantly, Bob agreed, and called Headquarters. Jupiter sighed when he heard Bob's bad news.

"Pete's been waylaid too," the First Investigator said. "He has to clean out his room. He promised to come over when he's done. Get here as soon as you can, Records."

Bob hurried to get his rags and window cleaner and go to work on the windows. He worked fast, but there were a lot of windows. It was almost eleven o'clock when he finally finished. He put away the cleaner, threw the rags into the hamper, and ran out to his bike.

"Don't forget, Bob," his father called after him. "I have to leave in about an hour!"

"OK, Dad!" Bob cried, and raced away on his bicycle.

As he came out of the driveway he had to swerve to pass a battered white pick-up truck that was parked directly in front of his house. It surprised him because there was almost never anything parked in front of his house. Ever since the Smashing Glass mystery, his mother and father had parked their cars in the garage. He was so intent on not toppling over, he missed seeing who was in the driver's seat of the truck.

At the corner he glanced back. The pick-up had driven away from the kerb and was moving slowly behind him. He could hear the dilapidated truck squeaking and clanking.

He pedalled faster and turned some corners rapidly. When he looked back once more, the pick-up was still driving slowly behind him. He tried to see its licence plate, but it didn't have one in front.

Alarmed, he pedalled on as fast as he could, looking over his shoulder from time to time to see if the dented white truck was still following. It was.

Bob thought hard. He was almost at the salvage yard now, and if he was being followed, it probably meant that someone wanted to know where he was going, or find where the Three Investigators had their headquarters, or both. Bob decided he'd better stay away from the junk-yard and phone ahead to Jupe and Pete.

He turned into the last cross street before the salvage yard and stopped at a garage where there was an outside public telephone. Quickly he dialled the phone number of the Investigators' private telephone in Headquarters.

There was no answer!

Disappointed, Bob hung up. Pete and Jupe weren't there.

He stepped out of the booth and looked up and down the street. The white pick-up was nowhere in sight. He walked all around to be sure the truck was gone. Maybe it hadn't been following him after all. Maybe it was just a coincidence.

Bob got back on his bike and rode one block past the salvage yard. He saw no further sign of the pick-up. It seemed safe to head back to the yard.

Warily, he biked around to the rear fence of the junk yard. An enormous mural of the fire caused by the San Francisco Earthquake of 1906 had been painted there years ago. It was full of burning buildings and horse-drawn fire engines and people escaping with their possessions on their backs. About fifteen metres from the corner, a little dog had been painted looking sadly at a collapsed building that had been his home.

Bob looked carefully around once more to be sure the pick-up was not following him, then picked out a knot that was one of the little dog's eyes. He reached inside quickly, lifted a catch, and swung three boards up. This was Red Gate Rover, one of the boys' secret entrances to the salvage yard. Bob was sure no one saw him enter.

Completely hidden from the yard office or the front gate, he parked his bike and got down on his hands and knees. A stack of building materials directly in front of him formed a cavelike opening. Bob crawled under the pile and emerged in a narrow tunnel between stacks of junk. This was the pathway to Door Four, one of four secret ways into headquarters – the Three Investigators' base of operations. The approach to Door Four was so narrow and tortuous that the chubby First Investigator rarely used it. He might get stuck!

The passage twisted and turned until Bob had to get down on his hands and knees again. He crawled a few feet, stood up, and knocked on a panel once . . . twice . . . three times.

If Jupe and Pete were inside, the panel would open. If not . . .

The panel opened!

He stepped inside the old house trailer that was Head-quarters. Hidden under mounds of junk and forgotten by everyone else, the secret headquarters was equipped with a darkroom, special lab, desk, typewriter, telephone, tape recorder, telephone-answering machine, and a host of other pieces of equipment Jupiter had managed to repair or build from salvage-yard junk.

"Where were you two? I called, but no one answered."

"We made the mistake of going out to the workshop," Pete said in disgust. "Aunt Mathilda saw us and got us both to move furniture."

Jupiter was watching Bob. "What's happened, Records? Why did you call us?"

Bob told them about the bashed-in white pick-up. Jupe and Pete listened intently.

"You don't know who was in the truck?" Pete asked.

"Nope, I couldn't catch a glimpse of the driver."

"Are you sure it was following you?" Jupiter asked.

"I was sure until I turned off to call you," Bob said. "When I went back to the street, it was gone. Maybe it just looked like it was tailing me."

"Perhaps," Jupiter mused, frowning, "but we will all keep our eyes open. Now, what about the film?"

"I almost forgot!" Bob cried, looked at their clock on the wall. It was almost eleven thirty. "I've got to get them to my dad in half an hour!"

"We can't develop two rolls in half an hour," Pete said.

"Dad says to just give him the film – he'll get it developed at his newspaper."

"That," Jupiter declared, "will not be necessary. While you two were working this morning, I developed both rolls. The negatives are quite dry now, so you can take them to your father instead of prints."

"Where are they?"

Jupiter went into the darkroom and returned with all the negatives in a brown manila envelope. Bob grabbed it and pushed open the panel of Door Four.

"I'll be back as soon as I get them to Dad."

The Records and Research man ran bent-over through the narrow passage, crawled out to his bike, and left the junk yard through Red Gate Rover.

He turned the first corner and rode up to the main road that passed in front of the salvage yard. As he turned left towards his house, he heard a motor start. Bob shot a startled glance over his shoulder.

The white pick-up truck was there!

5

A Moving Target

Bob had a quick glimpse of two heads in the white pick-up before he rode away as fast as he could, keeping close to the kerb.

The pick-up was right behind him!

He pedalled hard, but the truck drew closer until it was just behind his rear wheel. He tried to crane his head around to see the face of at least one of the people up in the cab, but all he saw was the radiator grille.

The truck stayed just behind him, moving slowly along at the same pace he was riding his bicycle, as if waiting for something.

Bob saw that the block ahead had no houses along it – only gardens on one side and a small park with trees and bushes and paths on the other. Suddenly he knew this was what his pursuers were waiting for – an empty block.

He began to ride through the deserted block. The truck moved up and started turning in front of him to cut him off!

He slammed on his brakes.

Surprised, the truck shot ahead, screeching to a stop as it almost went off the road.

Bob had a brief glimpse of a grimy California licence plate that began with "56" before he turned on to a path and rode into the park. He pedalled around the curves to the opposite exit on the far side.

He glanced behind him only once. No one was following.

He shot out into the street parallel to the one he had been biking on and turned back the way he had come, towards the salvage yard instead of away from it. A large station wagon came up behind him, blocking him from view. He looked back and grinned as the pick-up appeared at the far corner and turned the wrong way.

When he was sure the two men in the pick-up could not see him, he turned again and pedalled on across another street before resuming the trip towards his house.

Then he heard it. The motor, the sudden squeaks and rattles. He looked wildly over his shoulder. The pick-up was behind him once more!

This time it came next to him fast, not waiting, and swerved in hard against his rear wheel. Bob wobbled and hung on desperately as he pedalled.

The pick-up swerved in again.

Bob saw the deep ditch along the edge of the road, felt his bike going over, and jumped.

Dimly aware that the truck was stopping, he landed at the bottom of the ditch, tumbled forward and rolled up on to his feet. His shirt and pants were torn, his hands and knees scraped and covered with dirt, but he didn't stop or look back. He ran along the ditch and then scrambled out near a house. He breathed hard and listened. He heard no sound of pursuit. No running, no shouts.

He looked back. The yard he stood in, the ditch, and the road were deserted. He saw his bike a half block back lying at the edge of the ditch, but that was all he saw. No one was trying to attack him, no one was even chasing him. The white pick-up truck was gone!

Momentarily puzzled, he suddenly began to feel in his pockets and stare at his empty hands. Where was the manila envelope?

He hurried back down into the ditch and walked carefully along it to the spot where he had jumped off his bicycle. There was no envelope.

He climbed up to the road. His bike was there, lying on its side.

The envelope was gone.

They had stolen all the negatives!

He should have realized what they wanted and protected the envelope better! He wasn't sure how he would have done that, but he blamed himself as he picked up his bike. Then he shook himself out of his self-pity. As Jupiter always said, worrying about what had already happened didn't help anything. What Bob had to do now was think about how to get the negatives back!

He jumped on his bike and rode quickly towards the salvage yard. He rode straight in through the main gate this time. There was no more need to conceal his destination. The white pick-up was gone.

Bob walked quickly to a corner of the yard where Jupiter had set up an outdoor workshop. This was where he repaired the gadgets that became the Investigators' detection equipment. The Records and Research man made for a piece of iron grating that was leaning casually against the opening of a large corrugated pipe. This pipe was actually Tunnel Two, another of the boys' secret entrances to Headquarters. Bob slid through the pipe as quickly as his skinned bones would allow and came out under a trap door in the floor of Headquarters. As he pushed up through the trap door, Pete and Jupiter gazed at him in astonishment.

"That was fast work, Records," Pete said.

Jupiter saw Bob's torn shirt and pants and the dirt stains on his hands. "You were attacked by the people in that white pick-up!"

"No, just run off the road. But they got the negatives," Bob cried miserably. "All of them!"

"Did you see who they were?" Jupiter asked quickly.

"We won't get paid!" Pete wailed.

"Tell us exactly what happened, Records," Jupiter demanded.

Bob told them about having his bike rammed. "I think

there were two of them. I never got a clear look, and all I could see of the licence was that it was a California plate that began with fifty-six. We've got to get those negatives back."

"Without the licence," Pete said, "and no idea who they are, how can we?"

"It would take days anyway," Bob moaned. He looked at his watch. "And Dad has to leave for the office in half an hour."

Jupiter nodded. "Bob is quite right. He must get the pictures to Mr Andrews first, then deal with our thieves."

Bob and Pete stared at him.

"But-but, Jupe," Pete stammered, "the thieves *have* the pictures."

"They got them all, Jupe," Bob pointed out.

"No," Jupiter said with a grin, "not quite all. It just happens that I had nothing to do all morning, so I printed out a complete set of photos. The prints were still wet when you arrived, Bob, so I just gave you the negatives."

The First Investigator went into the darkroom and came out with the set of photos in his hand. They were still damp. Pete let out a whoop, and Bob jumped with excitement.

"Awesome! Let's get them to my dad!"

"Wait!" Pete cried. "Let's look and see why those thieves wanted them so badly!"

He grabbed the prints and spread them out quickly on the desk. Bob and Jupiter leaned closely on either side of the tall Second Investigator and peered down at the prints. There were forty-eight of them and they filled the desk to overflowing. Each of the boys began to shake his head.

"I don't see anything except the Indians and Vikings and their battle," Bob said.

"Even in the close-ups you took, all I can see is them and their picnic," Pete agreed.

Jupiter nodded slowly. "From the first shots out on the ocean, all I can see is what we saw with our bare eyes. But these photos must have captured something those thieves didn't want others to see."

"Like what they were making for lunch?" Pete joked.

"Maybe they just wanted the pictures for themselves," Bob said. "As souvenirs."

"Enough to run you off the road and perhaps injure you?" the First Investigator asked. "It doesn't make sense."

"Hey, maybe it was that Sam Ragnarson!" Bob exclaimed.

"That already occurred to me, Records," Jupiter said. "But we had better get these prints to your dad. We'll ask him to make duplicates for us, then we can study them a lot closer."

"Sure, Jupe," Bob agreed. "The lab in Dad's office can have the duplicates for us tonight."

They slid the prints into another manila envelope and crawled out through Tunnel Two to their bikes. This time they rode to Bob's house without incident. Bob's father was just about to get into his car in the driveway.

"I'd given up on you, Bob," Mr Andrews said, nodding at the manila envelope Jupiter had in his hand. "Are those the pictures? I told Bob not to take the time to develop them – you almost missed me."

"I'd already developed them, sir," Jupiter explained. "That isn't why we're late."

Bob told his father about the attack by the two men in the white pick-up. "So that's the only set of prints, Dad. Could you make us copies at your office?"

"All right," Mr Andrews said. "I'll use this set for the story and have the lab make up another set for you."

"We'd appreciate it, sir," Jupiter told him. "We want to find out why those two men are so desperate to have these photos."

Mr Andrews laughed. "Bob could be exaggerating what happened, boys. You know he's always got his head into mystery stories. Those people out on the island probably just wanted the photos and were trying to ask Bob for them, and he thought they were chasing him."

Jupiter sighed and exchanged sympathetic glances with the other Investigators. By now he was used to adults thinking the boys were just playing at cops and robbers.

"Perhaps, sir . . ." the leader of the team began.

Bob was furious. "They were trying to run me off the road, Dad! I'm *not* exaggerating."

"Well, maybe." Mr Andrews grinned infuriatingly. "But I'd better get these to my office or the publisher will be running *me* off the paper! I'll bring your prints home tonight."

Mr Andrews climbed into his car and backed slowly out of the driveway. When the car had vanished along the quiet residential street towards the motoway and Los Angeles, Bob rolled his eyes.

"Adults!" he sputtered. 'Sometimes . . . though Dad did tell me something interesting stuff about Ragnarson Rock."

Jupiter turned to his two companions and checked his watch. "I've come to some conclusions," he declared. "One, Bob has had a harrowing morning and deserves lunch. Two, the Three Investigators' treasury is not too depleted to treat us all to pizza – "

"Pepperoni with extra cheese?" Pete interrupted.

Jupe nodded, continuing, "As I was saying, Bob can fill us in about Ragnarson Rock over lunch. And three, afterwards we have something to settle with Sam Ragnarson."

6

An Odd Encounter

Sam Ragnarson's address turned out to be a dilapidated cottage near the beach at the upper end of Rocky Beach. The once green paint had peeled and turned grey from salt spray and neglect, and the small porch sagged. The front and side yards were a thick jungle of overgrown hibiscus, bougainvillea, trumpet vine, pittosporum, and different cacti.

"Boy," Pete said, "he sure isn't much of a gardener."

"Or a housepainter or carpenter," Bob added.

Jupiter studied the ramshackle dwelling distastefully. "It certainly is a mess. But there seems to be something like a garage at the rear. I suggest we look there for the white pick-up before confronting Sam Ragnarson."

They left their bikes chained to a fence next door and slipped quickly around the side of the house, through the dense garden foliage, to the garage. Unpainted, some of its boards already rotted, the garage was in worse condition than the cottage itself. There were wide gaps between some of the leaning boards. The boys peered inside.

"Fellows!" Pete cried. "I see a pick-up truck! And it's all dented and rusty!"

"You're right, Second." Jupiter nodded. "Is it the truck that followed you, Records?"

Bob shaded his eyes against the outside sunlight and stared intently into the garage. "It's the wrong colour. This one's kind of a pale brown. The one that chased me was flat white. It's shaped differently too. Besides, look at the licence. It doesn't begin with fifty-six."

"Well," Pete said reluctantly, "he drives a pick-up anyway. Maybe he's got another one."

"There is room for another vehicle in the garage," Jupiter said thoughtfully. "He might have sent some friends in another truck to steal the negatives. Come on."

They retraced their steps to the front yard and climbed the steps to the sagging porch. Inside the two filthy front windows were filmy, spotted curtains. Jupiter pushed the doorbell. There was no ring. He tried again.

"The doorbell's probably broken." Bob grinned. "Everything else is around here."

"It would not surprise me," Jupiter agreed.

The stout leader of the team knocked on the door. The boys waited. There was no answer. Jupiter knocked harder.

"I guess he's not at home," Jupiter said. "We'll have to come back."

Pete was trying to see in through the dirt and curtains of a window. "Wait, First! I think I see something moving in there."

"Are you sure, Second?" Jupiter said, peering in.

The dim interior was as cluttered and broken as the exterior and garage. They could see upholstered chairs with the stuffing coming out. Springs stuck out of a tattered couch. A long table, some dusty wooden chairs, torn rugs piled in corners . . . everything was bent or broken or leaning in the dim light.

"Look all the way to the back," Pete instructed.

Through the dirty windows, the curtains, and the interior gloom they seemed to see someone, or something, moving around in a back room. Whoever – or whatever – was inside, he was acting very peculiar. He would wave his arms, then freeze and look off to the side. Then crouch and look, then lean forward as if to pounce. His movements were stilted – like the jerky motions of actors in old films.

"Wh-what is it?" Pete stuttered. "I just remembered I have a date with a hamburger."

"Is it Sam Ragnarson?" Bob whispered.

Pete shaded his eyes against the reflection on the window. "Whatever that thing is, it's wearing some kind of uniform."

"Actually," Jupiter said as he peered inside, "we don't really know what Sam Ragnarson looks like. The only time we saw him he was wearing that bulky Viking costume."

"That's no Viking," Pete stated.

"The real question," Jupiter said, "is why he doesn't come to the door."

"Maybe he can't hear us," Bob suggested. "Too involved in whatever he's doing back there."

"Maybe he doesn't want to hear us," Pete said ominously. "Maybe he doesn't want to open the door. Maybe h-he's not right in his mind."

"You mean" – Bob gulped – "like someone is going crazy in there . . ."

Jupiter said matter-of-factly, "I suggest we go around to the back again and find out what *is* in that back room."

The rear windows were all boarded up. There was no way to see inside.

"What do we do now?" Pete said.

"Well" – Jupiter looked at the boarded windows and the closed rear door – "I see no choice but to knock on the back door as loud as we can and see if he will answer."

Pete swallowed. "Are you sure we want him to?"

"I'm sure," the leader of the trio said firmly. "We must ascertain if anything has happened to Sam Ragnarson and where he is."

Against his better judgment, Pete began to knock on the rear door with the other two. No one answered.

Jupiter called out, "Is Mr Sam Ragnarson in there?"

"We have to talk to him about our photos!" Bob yelled.

39

"We – " Pete began.

The back door flung open with a crash, and the man stood framed in the dim light inside the doorway, glaring at them.

"Ye'll stop the ringing and banging and yelling, or I'll have ye whipped at the mainmast."

He was a thin man with a high, sneering voice and a bushy white moustache. His pale blue eyes stared at them from under a small-visored navy-blue cap with gold braid. He wore a tight-fitting dark blue coat that had a high stiff collar and shiny brass buttons down to his knees. He had on narrow blue trousers, ankle-high laced black boots, and white gloves. He carried a brass telescope.

"We wish to speak to Mr Sam Ragnarson," Jupiter said in his most aristocratic voice.

"Ain't here."

The man turned away and walked off into the house.

"We want to know if he's got another pick-up truck!" Bob blurted out.

"A white one, all battered," Pete insisted.

The man didn't bother to turn. "He ain't."

"It is possible, my good man, that Sam Ragnarson stole some valuable photographs." The stocky leader of the trio always put on his most lordly manner whenever an adult became arrogant with the boys. "If he did, he could be in great trouble."

The man in the long blue coat stopped. One cold eye looked back over his shoulder at the boys. "Ye'll be having a care who ye accuse of a crime, me buckos. Sam Ragnarson's a true Viking. He's not to be trifled with, ye hear? Now be off wi' ye, or I'll have ye keelhauled!"

With that, the menacing stranger slammed the back door in the boys' faces.

"He sure is unfriendly." Pete stared at the closed door.

"Yes," Jupiter agreed, "and I wonder why. We were just making routine inquiries."

40

"So what do we do now, First?" Pete asked. "Wait around for Sam Ragnarson? He could be off on his rock and not be back for hours."

"I think," Jupiter said, "it's time for some research into the Ragnarsons and Ragnarson Rock. Second, you go to the local newspaper and the Chamber of Commerce, and find out all you can about the Ragnarson family."

"I'll go to the Historical Museum and look up the Ragnarsons and the Rock," Bob said.

"OK, then I'll go to the library," Jupiter concluded. "Sam Ragnarson may or may not have stolen our negatives, but he certainly wanted them, and I want to know why."

7

A Live Ghost!

Pete Crenshaw rubbed his neck and groaned as he came out of the building housing the *Rocky Beach News*, a small weekly paper that came out every weekend. He had spent the whole afternoon in offices, and he hated indoor work. He took deep breaths of the late afternoon air off the Pacific Ocean and rode slowly to the salvage yard, happy to be out in the open doing something physical after all the reading and talking to people.

Only Jupe's bike was in the outdoor workshop. Pete crawled through Tunnel Two and up into their hidden headquarters.

"Bob not here yet?"

"I expect he had a lot more to read at the Historical Museum than we did. What did you find out about the Ragnarson family?"

"I found out there's a lot of them," Pete said. "George Ragnarson owns that big hardware store downtown, and Mr Karl Ragnarson, of course, is our school principal. Dr Ingmar Ragnarson is a dentist in town. The dentist is Sam's father. There are two engineers who work down in Los Angeles, and an accountant who works up in Ventura. Then there are a bunch of others who live around the state and come up here for a week for the reunion battle. I copied down all the addresses of the ones in Rocky Beach. Everyone says the Ragnarsons are good, reliable people. All except Sam, that is."

"What about Sam?" Jupiter said quickly.

"He's the black sheep of the family. He dropped out of high school and became a beach bum. He's twenty-two and has never held a steady job. Sam's always trying out shady schemes to make money. He was in juvenile hall a couple of times, and almost went to jail once because of some get-rich-quick con. From what everyone says, he's trouble – if not worse. Always trying to make a buck without working."

"At the library I didn't learn much more than Bob's dad told him," Jupiter countered. "Knut Ragnarson did so well selling boots in 1849 that he decided to bring back his family from Illinois. He took a passage on *The Star of Panama*. It was supposed to sail to Panama. Then the passengers would cross the isthmus – there wasn't any canal then – and get another ship on the Atlantic side. Only its captain, a man named Henry Coulter, had other ideas. *The Star of Panama* had a cargo of gold going back East. There were coins and nuggets and gold dust. When the ship was off Rocky Beach, he put all the gold in the longboat, opened the sea cocks to flood the ship and sink it, and rowed away with the crew."

"Gosh, he was nothing but a thief and a murderer! How was he going to get away with it, First?" Pete wondered. "I mean, what was he going to say happened?"

"I expect he intended to claim that the ship sank and the gold went down with it," Jupiter said. "He nearly got away with it. The passengers were asleep and no one escaped drowning that night except Knut Ragnarson. He only survived because he liked to sleep up on deck and, as Bob told us, managed to reach Ragnarson Rock on a hatch cover."

"Boy, he sure was lucky," Pete said.

Jupiter nodded. "He was very lucky, and he got even luckier. The island's not much more than a big treeless rock, no food or animals or water or anything. If he hadn't found a Chumash plank canoe and paddled it to the mainland, he'd have died on the rock. Captain Coulter had made sure he sank *The Star of Panama* way out of the usual ship lanes."

"What happened to Captain Coulter and his men?" Pete wondered.

"I don't know, Second. I found nothing about that in the library. But I did find out that thirty years ago, old Knut's grandson Sven – who lives up north – rediscovered the rock and decided to celebrate his grandfather's good fortune by having a family picnic and mock battle every five years. The Chumash canoe gave him the idea of having a 'fight' between Indians and Vikings to claim the Rock. The Chumash never really had any wars. The Ragnarsons all liked the idea, and they've been doing it ever since."

The voice startled both of them. "Well, shiver my timbers!"

They whirled and saw Bob, laughing, climb up through the trap door from Tunnel Two. They had been so engrossed in the story of *The Star of Panama*, they hadn't heard the Records and Research man open the trap door.

"Good grief, Records!" Pete exclaimed once he caught his breath. "Don't *do* things like that!"

Bob climbed up and closed the door behind him.

"Did you learn what happened to Captain Coulter?" Jupe asked.

"Nope," Bob said. "No one ever saw him, or his crew, or the gold again! They just vanished."

Bob told them all he had learned at the Historical Museum. It was essentially what Jupiter had learned at the library. "By the time Knut Ragnarson got to shore," Bob continued, "there was no trace of the captain or of the gold. No one had seen the captain and his crew come ashore or anything. They decided he must have waited out at sea and been picked up by another ship. They figured he might even have waited on the little island itself, and that's why they gave it another name: Wreckers' Rock!"

Jupiter was listening intently. "You mean it's possible

Captain Coulter and Knut Ragnarson were both on the island at the same time?"

"That's what some people back then thought," Bob said.

"Then it's possible that if one of them had any secrets, the other discovered them," the First Investigator concluded. 'Good work, Records. Is that all?"

"Not exactly." Bob took a folded piece of paper from his jacket pocket. "I found something else too. They let me make a photocopy of it."

He held up a copy of a large photograph – a very old photograph of a man standing tall and stiff. "It's called a daguerreotype. You had to stand very still for a long time while it was taken."

But the other two boys weren't even listening to him. They stared at the photocopied photograph. It showed a tall, thin man in a knee-length, high-collared, dark coat with brass buttons. He had a bristling white moustache and pale eyes under a small-visored navy cap with gold braid. He wore narrow pants, laced boots and white gloves and carried a brass telescope.

"It's that man we saw – " Pete began.

"At Sam Ragnarson's house!" Jupiter finished.

"And he is also," Bob added, "Captain Henry Coulter of *The Star of Panama*!"

"Th-the captain of *Th-the Star of Panama*?" Pete stammered.

Jupiter stared at Bob. "Are you sure, Records? Where did that picture come from?"

"It's in a book about unsolved California crimes. The whole story of *The Star of Panama* is in it. That's where I found out no one ever saw Captain Coulter or his crew again."

"But," Pete said in a small voice, "that happened over a hundred years ago! The captain would be at least . . ."

"It happened almost a hundred and fifty years ago,

45

Second," Jupiter calculated, "and that would make Captain Coulter around a hundred and seventy. Sea captains were almost never under thirty in those days."

"Then," Pete said, "it couldn't have been Captain Coulter we saw!"

"Not alive, no," Bob answered.

Pete groaned. "I don't think I want to hear the rest."

"Certainly not alive," Jupiter agreed thoughtfully. "Therefore, we can make one of three possible deductions: we saw someone who just happened to resemble that picture; someone is impersonating Captain Coulter for some reason; or it was a ghost."

"I said I didn't want to hear the rest!" Pete repeated.

The other two ignored the nervous Second Investigator.

"It couldn't be someone who just happened to look like the picture, Jupe," Bob decided. "Nobody wears clothes like that today. Besides, he looked *exactly* like the picture. That's too much of a coincidence."

"Then it was an impersonation of the captain," Jupiter said.

"Or a real ghost," Bob said.

"Maybe Bob photographed the ghost," Pete suggested, "and that's why Sam Ragnarson wants our negatives. The ghost captured him on the Rock, and he's working under an evil spell!"

"Oh, come off it," Jupiter said impatiently. "Ghosts can't be photographed. Anyway, they don't even exist, so it must be someone impersonating the captain."

"Maybe ghosts can't be photographed," Pete muttered to himself, "but are very real anyway. Just invisible."

"Why would anyone want to impersonate the captain of *The Star of Panama*, Jupe?" Bob wondered.

Jupiter shook his head. "I don't know, Records. But it can't be a coincidence, as you said."

"Maybe Sam Ragnarson didn't steal the negatives,"

Bob ventured. "Maybe it was the man disguised as Captain Coulter who did it."

"It could have been Sam himself disguised as the captain," Jupiter pointed out. "But we don't know enough yet to have any real answers. We must investigate further and find out all we can about Sam and the other Ragnarsons."

"How, Jupe?" Bob asked.

"Tomorrow we will question the Ragnarsons."

"You think they're *all* up to something, Jupe?" Bob exclaimed.

"All we know, Records, is that Sam threatened us for the photos, two people stole your negatives, and someone seems to be impersonating the captain of *The Star of Panama*. I don't know why, but one thing does occur to me – you said neither the captain, his crew, nor the gold were ever found. Perhaps *The Star of Panama*'s gold is still out there on the Rock!"

8

Painful Interviews

Bob woke up late the next day. He was more tired than he had realized from being chased back and forth through Rocky Beach. When he made it down to the kitchen, a note was taped to the refrigerator:

Good morning, lazybones!

I was covering a forest fire up in the hills till late yesterday and I'm out early this morning. Sorry I missed you last night. I got in after you were in bed. And I didn't get back to the paper to pick up those duplicate prints for you. I *promise* I'll bring them home with me tonight.

Love,
Dad

P.S. Your mum is at the supermarket. She wants me to ask you to go to the cleaners', water the lawn . . .

Bob's eyes glazed over. He put the note down, fixed his breakfast, and then started doing the errands one by one. It was not until noon that he reached the salvage yard. Pete was sitting glumly in the outdoor workshop.

"Hans had to go to the dentist, so Uncle Titus needed Jupiter to help him and Konrad on the truck." Hans and Konrad were two Bavarian brothers who helped Jupe's uncle in the salvage yard.

"We could start without Jupe," Bob considered.

"I don't even know what questions to ask," Pete said.

"Maybe just who or what is out on that Rock?"

48

Pete frowned. "I think I hear a voice telling me that wouldn't be right. We'd better wait for Jupe."

They did some small repairs in the workshop and inside Headquarters. Then they lay around in their hidden office looking at the clock on the wall. Bob noticed the stack of copies of the morning newspaper that they'd saved because of the story with their names in it.

"Gosh," Bob said, "I forgot all about Mr Manning. I wonder if they've found him yet?"

Pete shook his head. "My dad says there isn't much chance out there for someone who couldn't swim."

Bob picked up the telephone. "I'm going to call Chief Reynolds and find out. Maybe William Manning got home OK after all."

He had to wait until Chief Reynolds got off another line before the chief's quiet voice came on.

"No, Bob, I'm afraid there isn't much hope. The Coast Guard has called off the search."

"Gosh, that's too bad," Bob said sadly.

Pete had been toying with their periscope while Bob was on the phone. It was a piece of stovepipe, rigged up with mirrors, that could be raised through the roof of Headquarters to survey the yard and surroundings.

Pete straightened with a jerk. "Jupe's back with the truck." Pete lowered the scope, and both boys were out in the yard in a flash.

"Help us unload, fellows!" the First Investigator panted.

Bob and Pete pitched in, and the truck was unloaded in no time. Uncle Titus seemed dumbfounded by the speed at which his treasures came off the truck. Uncle Titus collected unusual junk, and this trip was no exception. The boys unloaded eighty-six grand piano legs, parts of an abandoned roller coaster, thirty-one wig stands, and nine hamster cages. Minutes after the truck had arrived, the Investigators were on their bikes and riding out of the yard.

After a quick stop for burgers, Pete led the way downtown to the Central House & Hardware Store owned by George Ragnarson. It was an enormous establishment that occupied an entire block, having about the same relation to an ordinary hardware store that the Jones Salvage Yard did to an ordinary junk yard. George Ragnarson was in the back storeroom checking stock. A short, stout, and busy man, he went on working as he talked.

"Well, what can I do for you boys?"

Jupiter took the lead. "We're very interested in the story of Ragnarson Rock, sir. We're doing a school history project on it and we would appreciate anything you can tell us about what you discovered out there recently."

"Discovered?" George Ragnarson checked off more stock on his pad. "We didn't discover anything I know of, except that we're all getting older. Aches and pains after all those shenanigans, eh? Still, I wish I was out there with the rest of them now. But business is business."

"We heard you might have found some evidence of what happened to Captain Coulter," Jupiter went on innocently.

"Who?" George Ragnarson stared up at his shelves as he wrote on his pad.

"The captain of *The Star of Panama*, sir," Bob said.

"Oh, the ship they scuttled under old Knut. No, I don't know anything about him."

"Maybe your nephew Sam does," Pete blurted out.

George Ragnarson stopped writing and turned to scowl at the boys. "That dropout is no nephew of mine. I'm sorry to say he's my cousin, and if you guys have anything to do with him, I don't even want to talk to you!"

"No, sir," Jupiter put in quickly, "we hardly even know

him. We've simply heard he's been acting rather odd lately. Is he in any trouble you know about?"

"Trouble is Sam's first, last, and middle name! When isn't that arrogant bum in trouble?"

"We were thinking," Jupiter went on, "of something more definite, sir. Perhaps connected to the reunion."

George Ragnarson snorted. "Surprised he even went out with us. You know he worked for me one summer and had the nerve to complain to everyone I was cheap? Me! After I'd paid him and he'd spent most of the time sleeping here in the back room!"

"Then he hasn't been acting weird lately?' Pete said.

"He's not in any kind of trouble?" Bob asked.

"He's been weird all his life, and he's always in trouble," George Ragnarson said, but grudgingly conceded, "only I don't know of any mess he's in right now."

They thanked the store owner and left him muttering to himself about Sam Ragnarson. Outside, Pete directed them to the office of Dr Ingmar Ragnarson, Sam's father. Dr Ragnarson's dental office was in a new three-storey yellow brick building on a tree-lined and secluded side street.

The receptionist greeted them with a smile. "Well now, all three of you boys can't have a toothache. Which one is it?

"Not me!" Pete exclaimed.

"None of us is a patient," Bob told her.

"We would like to speak to the doctor about his son," Jupiter explained. "If he can give us a few minutes."

"Which son would that be, boys?"

"Sam," Pete said.

She sighed. "I was afraid of that. It usually is Sam. Just a moment, then."

The receptionist pushed buttons, picked up a telephone, and spoke quietly into the receiver. Moments later a tall blond man in a white jacket came out of the inner offices. He looked unhappy.

"What's he done now, boys?"

He had a craggy, windburned face and, with his slightly long blond hair, looked like he should be sailing a real Viking ship.

"We don't know that he's done anything, Dr Ragnarson," Jupiter said solemnly. "Perhaps we could have a few minutes of your time to ask some questions."

"Don't I know you boys?" He looked at each of them closely, a puzzled expression on his face. Then he brightened and snapped his fingers. "Of course, you're the boys who took pictures of us out on the Rock! How did they come out?"

"Pretty well," Bob said. "They're one of the things we want to ask you about."

"All right, come on in."

He led them into a typical dentist's office with a reclining patient's chair and chrome dental equipment. In the chair was another blond man, a white smock protecting his clothes.

"This is my brother Karl, boys. He knows almost as much about Sam as I do, don't you, Karl?"

The three boys nodded to their junior high school principal.

"We know Mr Karl, sir," Bob said. "We go to his school."

"So did Sam," Mr Karl stated. He winced and put his hand to his jaw. "Are we going to be all day about this tooth, Ingmar? I'd like to get back out to the Rock for dinner, anyway."

"The boys here have some questions about Sam," Dr Ragnarson said. "But we can talk while I work, eh?" The dentist bent over Mr Karl and began working on his mouth. "Just why are you interested in Sam, boys?"

Jupiter gave the same story of doing a special school

paper on the Ragnarson family, and of hearing that Sam had been acting strangely and could be in some kind of trouble.

"Sam is always doing something strange," Dr Ragnarson observed, "but he hasn't been in serious trouble for years. Right, Karl?"

"*Garrrggh-ruggghhhh*," the school principal emitted with Dr Ragnarson's hands, mirror, and metal pick in his mouth.

"Oops. Sorry, Karl," the dentist said.

Mr Karl glared at his brother. "Not since he was in juvenile hall the last time. He's a bit of a rogue, but he usually hurts himself more than anyone else."

"Sam is what we used to call a maverick," Dr Ragnarson went on, getting out a large Novocain hypodermic, "but there's no real harm in him, is there, Karl."

"You might get a difference of opinion on that." The school principal looked nervously at the long steel needle. "But I agree that his bark is probably a lot worse than his bite."

"We already did get a different opinion from Mr George Ragnarson," Pete put in.

Dr Ragnarson shook his head. "George never will forgive Sam for chasing his boy up a tree when they were both about ten. As for the job story, which I'm sure he told you, for the salary that that skinflint cousin of mine pays, I'd sleep as much as I could, too."

As if to emphasize his point, the doctor suddenly inserted the hypodermic needle into Mr Karl's gum and pushed the plunger.

"*Aaahhhhhhhhh!*" Mr Karl cried, holding tightly to the arms of the chair. Then he said shakily, "George isn't known for his generosity."

"He's the only Ragnarson who doesn't take a week off for the reunion," Dr Ragnarson told them. "Comes over once or twice."

"Why aren't you both out there now?" Jupiter asked.

"Emergency. While we were out there, Karl got a toothache."

Loud voices came from out in the waiting room. Someone was arguing with the receptionist. Mr Karl seemed to listen to the noise for a moment, then looked at the boys.

"Do you have anything specific in mind, boys?" the school principal asked slowly, his voice already thickening as the Novocain numbed his mouth.

"We heard peculiar things were happening on the Rock," Bob guessed.

"Where did – ?" Dr Ragnarson began.

The sullen-looking young man who slammed into the office was thin and not much taller than Pete. He wore ragged jeans and a dirty T-shirt. He was barefoot and needed a shave.

"Dad . . ." he saw the Three Investigators and stopped with his mouth gaping open. "What are *they* doing here? Making wild accusations, I bet. I just wanted to buy their photos. If they tell you anything else, they're liars."

"Photos?" Dr Ragnarson repeated. "Why would you want to buy their pictures, Sam?"

The young man's face reddened. "I-I was going to surprise everyone, give them out as souvenirs."

Out of his shaggy Viking costume, horned helmet, and fake beard, Sam Ragnarson seemed younger and a lot smaller.

"Whah wouldth the boyth lie abou', Tham?" the school principal mumbled.

"That I got rough and pushed them around!" Sam snapped. "I didn't do a thing to them, Uncle Karl. I just wanted to buy the pictures for everyone." He grinned at his uncle ingratiatingly.

"If you didn't do anything," Dr Ragnarson said pointedly, "how do you know that they accused you of anything?"

Sam reddened again. "I . . . well . . . I can guess what kids like them would say."

Dr Ragnarson sighed. "You never were a good liar, Sam. As it happens, these boys haven't said anything against you. I'm afraid you've convicted yourself with your own protest."

Sam Ragnarson glared at the three boys.

"You oweth the boyth anth ap-p . . ." Mr Karl heroically tried to say through his numbed lips.

Dr Ragnarson grinned and got out his drill. 'Maybe you'd better not try to talk, Karl. Open up, and we'll get to work."

"An apology won't be necessary, sir," Jupiter said grimly. "And it's possible he's a lot worse than a liar. Our photographs were stolen yesterday. By two men in an old white pick-up truck. They ran Bob off the road and grabbed the negatives."

"I didn't steal anything!" Sam Ragnarson retorted angrily.

"You were the only one who wanted the photos!" Bob said.

"And you were in a big hurry," Jupiter added.

Sam was furious again. "You're liars!"

Dr Ragnarson looked worriedly at the boys. Mr Karl looked worriedly at the drill in the dentist's hand.

The dentist faced his son. "Are you sure, Sam? You seem to have wanted those photos."

"I don't even know where they live!"

Pete said, "He could have followed us home that night."

"I told him the photos were for my dad's newspaper," Bob pointed out. "And he heard my father's name. He could easily have tracked down where we live. The thieves were waiting in front of my house yesterday morning."

Dr Ragnarson looked even more worried. Mr Karl was sliding farther and farther down in the chair, his eyes fixed on the drill in the dentist's hand.

"I didn't steal anything," Sam repeated. "When were they stolen?"

The boys told him. Sam laughed, his face triumphant.

"I was out on the Rock then! Tell them, Dad!"

Dr Ragnarson nodded. "Yesterday Sam was with us on the Rock, boys. We came in together about eleven a.m., I remember."

"He could have had two pals of his do it!" Pete pursued.

"Now, boys, that's going too far," Dr Ragnarson objected, holding his drill poised over Mr Karl's waiting mouth.

"Tham theemth innocenth, boyth," Mr Karl managed from the chair. "Arr we gongha fixth thith fooff or noth!"

"You're probably right, sir," Jupiter said quietly, his round face bland and expressionless. "I'm sorry we've delayed your dental work. Come on, fellows, we'll have to look elsewhere for our thief."

Dr Ragnarson switched on the electric drill.

Jupiter hurriedly pushed Bob and Pete ahead of him, and they left the office and reception room. Once outside, Bob turned to the chubby leader of the trio.

"Why'd you give in so easy, First?"

"You think he didn't take the photos, Jupe?" Pete asked.

"It's possible, Second," Jupiter admitted, "but I'm not convinced yet. What we must find out is exactly why Sam *did* want our photos so badly. If Sam took the negatives, there must be something in them he doesn't want anyone to see."

The First Investigator checked his watch.

"It's after four. I propose we go to Bob's house – his father will be bringing home our duplicate prints any time now."

Pete was on his bike. "Let's go, then! The sooner we nab that Sam Ragnarson, the better I'll like it."

The three boys biked away along the quiet side street towards Bob's house. With Pete in the lead, Jupiter behind him, and Bob bringing up the rear, they pedalled steadily through the back streets of the town.

"Fellows!' Bob cried.

They looked behind them. Sam Ragnarson had just pulled into the nearest intersection on a motorcycle. He was glaring at them furiously.

"I'll teach you pests not to mess with me!" he spat out.

9

The Masked Men

The three boys pedalled as fast as they could, but the motorcycle roared up behind them, cut in, and sent Bob and his bicycle sprawling on a lawn.

"Not again!" yelled Bob.

"One!" Sam Ragnarson shouted, scowling.

He raced on past Jupe and Pete, whirled the motorcycle around, and roared straight back at the two boys. Jupiter quickly steered his bike off the road, wobbled across a bumpy path, through a grove of tall eucalyptus trees, and finally fell into a thick pile of dusty eucalyptus leaves.

"Two!" Sam gloated.

Furious, Pete stopped his bike and turned to face Sam as he revved the motor to ride back once more. The Second Investigator picked up a fallen eucalyptus branch and waited astride his bike for Sam to attack. At the other end of the block, the angry youth hesitated, sizing up the thick branch and Pete's determined face.

"What do you think you're going to do with that, boy?" Sam cried across the distance.

"Whatever I can," Pete called back.

Sam laughed. "Well, two out of three isn't bad. From now on, you three stay home and play with your toys, you understand? Or you might find yourselves in real trouble."

With that final threat, Sam turned his motorcycle and roared off in the opposite direction. Pete dropped his tree limb and hurried back to his pals. Bob was limping up across the lawns of the houses and Jupiter was brushing leaves and dust from himself and his battered bike.

"That was bold, Second," Jupiter wheezed, sneezing

from the dust and heavy medicinal odour of the eucalyptus.

"He made me mad," Pete said. "Anyhow, are you guys OK?"

"My front wheel's a little bent, but I can ride it and fix it at home," Bob said. "This is not my week for biking."

"I'll smell like eucalyptus for some time to come," Jupiter observed, "but otherwise I seem unharmed. I suggest we continue on to Bob's house and . . . oooffff!"

The stout First Investigator fell flat into the pile of eucalyptus leaves again! Something had struck him in the back.

"Down!" Pete cried to Bob, and both boys dived to the ground.

"It's Sam again!" Bob cried.

Jupiter struggled to get up, puffing and flailing among the long, dusty leaves. In some ways he resembled a beached whale. Pete couldn't help grinning as he raised his head and looked up and down the street for their attacker. Then Pete stood up with a disgusted look on his face.

"It was just the newspaper!"

They all saw the newspaper boy bicycling away up the street, an apologetic grin on his face. Bob ran forward.

"It's my dad's paper! Let's see if the photos are in it!"

He picked up the folded newspaper that had knocked the wind out of Jupiter, quickly opened it, and spread it out on the pavement. Jupiter and Pete crowded around.

"Here it is!" Bob exclaimed.

They bent over the feature on the Ragnarson reunion and the mock battle on Ragnarson or Wreckers' Rock. Ignoring the now-familiar story, the boys pored over the six pictures that had been printed with the article.

They studied the photos of the mock Vikings and Chumash Indians as if they were looking for the stolen gold itself. Bob finally shook his head.

"I don't see anything Sam could be worried about. Just the whole gang laughing and running around like lunatics."

"Nothing," Pete agreed. "Unless he's worried about sea gulls and one fat seal over there to the left. Funny, I don't remember a seal out there."

"The camera often catches objects we don't notice at the time. We're too intent on watching something in particular and don't see what's off on the edge, but the camera does," Jupiter explained pontifically. Then he finished somewhat lamely, 'But I don't see anything either. Nothing but the Ragnarsons and the Rock and a lot of sky and ocean."

"Well," Bob said firmly, "the article shows only six of the photos. I took forty-eight, so maybe whatever Sam Ragnarson is after is in one of the others. Let's go over to my house and check out all of them when my dad gets home."

With Bob's front wheel wobbling, and Jupiter still sneezing from the dust and eucalyptus odour on his clothes, it was a slow journey to Bob's house. They watched in all directions for Sam Ragnarson, but the bad-tempered youth did not appear again. They finally reached Bob's block. As they turned in, a voice called loudly from somewhere in the middle of the block.

"What do you two think you're doing! Get away from me!"

"It's my dad!" Bob cried.

Up the street, in the driveway leading to Bob's house, Mr Andrews stood against his car with two masked men confronting him! He was holding a large yellow-and-black envelope marked PHOTOS.

"Come on!" Pete cried. "They're after the photos again!"

The tall Second Investigator dropped his bike and ran toward Mr Andrews and the two ski-masked attackers.

Bob came close behind, and Jupiter puffed in the rear as they pounded up the tree-lined street. One of the masked men heard them coming and glanced quickly over his shoulder.

"Help!" Pete shouted as he ran. "Help, everybody! Yell, fellows!"

"Help!" Bob yelled.

Mr Andrews heard the boys and stopped struggling for a moment. One of the masked men grabbed the envelope of photos from his hand, and the two men dashed across the street towards a battered white pick-up that waited with its engine running. Pete was as close to the pick-up as the attackers were. He veered at an angle as he ran, and made a flying tackle of the man with the envelope. Bob, right behind the Second Investigator, piled on top of them.

"Help, everyone!" Jupiter shouted.

Windows and doors opened all along the quiet street. Neighbours began to emerge. The masked men flung off Pete and Bob and jumped into the pick-up. Before anyone could do anything more, the truck roared off with a squeal of tyres, screeched around the far corner, and was gone.

"The photos!" Jupiter panted.

Pete held up the big yellow-and-black envelope in triumph. "They didn't get them this time!"

Bob slapped him on the shoulder. "Good work, Second!"

"Dad, are you all right?" Bob cried, running up to his father.

"I'm fine," Mr Andrews said, "but what the heck was that all about?"

"It's what I was trying to tell you yesterday," Bob explained, exasperated. "They're after those photos I took on Ragnarson Rock."

Mr Andrews nodded ruefully. "Sorry I didn't really believe you till now, Bob."

"Oh, that's OK, Dad. Just tell us what happened."

Mr Andrews tried to reconstruct the events of the last half-hour.

"I noticed that old wreck of a truck when I drove up to the house today. I didn't think anything of it. I had the duplicate prints I promised to bring you. I got out of the car carrying the photo envelope and those heavies grabbed me."

"Did anyone get that licence plate number?" Mr Andrews asked.

"Gosh no, Dad," Bob admitted.

"It was covered with mud," Pete reported, "and I didn't get much of a look at them either. But I did see one thing: one of those guys has a mermaid tattooed on his left arm!"

"A good clue, Second," Jupiter said.

The boys asked all the neighbours if anyone had noticed the licence or seen anything special about the two masked men. No one had. Only that one was taller than the other, and they wore old jeans, work shirts, and heavy boots. The ski masks had covered their entire faces, so no one could describe them.

"And they said nothing to me," Mr Andrews explained. "Just jumped out of that pick-up and tried to get the envelope. They looked pretty muscular, but that's all I saw."

The neighbours slowly drifted away, and the boys went back to get their bikes and follow Mr Andrews into his house. Mrs Andrews examined them all for cuts or bruises and found only a small scrape on Pete's arm. When she'd treated the scrape with antiseptic, she pronounced the boys uninjured.

"Let's get a look at those prints," Jupe urged, "before something else happens."

Bob and Pete opened the envelope and spread the forty-eight duplicate prints all around the living room coffee table and chairs.

Mr Andrews came into the living room.

"I just called the police," he said, "and they'll be here shortly. Unless there's something they should see in the photographs, please pick them up and find another place to work."

"Right," said Jupe. "We'll take them over to Headquarters."

The boys gathered up the prints and hurried out to their bikes once more. Bob had forgotten about his bent wheel, but now found a spare in the garage. While he was replacing the wheel, Jupiter looked preoccupied.

"What's wrong, Jupe?" Pete wondered.

"Something just doesn't fit," the leader of the trio said. "The only way those two masked men could have known they didn't get everything we had when they stole all forty-eight negatives was to have seen the afternoon paper. But Sam Ragnarson was with us at his father's office and then when he tried to scare us off, so how could he have seen the paper in time to send his cohorts here before we got here?"

"He couldn't have," Bob said as he tightened the replacement wheel into position. "That paper we saw is the first edition. He'd have to have contacted his pals and sent them to get Dad after he tried to run us down, and there sure wouldn't have been enough time."

"So what does that mean, First?" Pete wondered.

"It means either Sam saw the paper way before we did or that someone else is after the photos!"

"Gosh, Jupe," Bob said. "Why would anyone else want them? I mean, all I did was take pictures of the reunion on the Rock."

"Yes, Records, why?" Jupiter's forehead knotted. Then his face cleared and his voice grew determined. "But the answer must be in those photos. All we have to do is find it."

Bob finished attaching his wheel and hopped on his bike.

"Then let's go and look at the photos, fellows!"

They pedalled rapidly back to the salvage yard with no further mishaps. As they rode through the gates and on towards their outdoor workshop, Aunt Mathilda came out of the office and shouted to them.

"All right, you young scamps. There's someone here who wants to talk to you. You're in real trouble this time!"

10

Scares in the Dark

The junior high school principal, Karl Ragnarson, came out of the office behind Aunt Mathilda.

"Now what have you boys done to bring your principal after you?" asked Aunt Mathilda. Her voice was stern, but there was a twinkle in her eye.

"If you don't mind, Mrs Jones," said Mr Ragnarson, "I would like to speak to the boys in private."

"I don't mind at all," Aunt Mathilda said, and grinned at the boys. "They can take you to that workshop they spend so much time hiding in. And don't let them sweet-talk you out of their just desserts!"

With a chuckle, she strode back into the office and closed the door. The boys led Karl Ragnarson to the outdoor workshop. The principal sat down on an old salvaged swivel chair and smiled at the boys. His grin was still a little lopsided from his dental work that afternoon.

"I'm sorry if I alarmed you boys, but I didn't want anyone to know why I'm here, not even your aunt."

"I bet it's about Sam, Mr Karl!" Pete exclaimed.

"I hope it isn't about Sam," Mr Karl replied. "But I must say I became concerned after you talked to us, because odd things *have* been happening out on the Rock!"

"What things?" Jupiter said eagerly.

"Well, first there have been strange noises the last two nights, like animals howling, and crazy laughter that no one admits to making. Then there have been 'ghosts' and weird lights coming from nowhere."

"What . . . kind of ghosts, Mr Karl?" Pete asked nervously.

"One seemed to look like a drowned man, all covered with seaweed, and the other was an old sea captain in a long uniform coat with brass – "

"Buttons down to his knees, tight trousers, and a small cap with gold braid on it!" Jupiter finished. "Even carrying a brass telescope, correct?"

"Yes, exactly!" Mr Karl gaped at the portly boy. "But how did you know that, Jupiter?"

"We've seen that ghost ourselves, sir," Jupiter said, and he told the principal about the man in Sam Ragnarson's cottage. "Are those all the peculiar occurrences, sir?"

The principal shook his head. "I'm afraid not. Things have also been disappearing. A torch, a hunting knife, some blankets, a down jacket, a camp stove, and quite a lot of food and even beer. Of course, the noises and the ghosts and the missing things are not necessarily connected, but they could be."

"And you think Sam could be stealing what's missing," Bob realized.

"Stealing and selling it." Mr Karl nodded. "When you came to see Ingmar, it occurred to me that you might have photographed Sam actually stealing something while we were all busy posing for your cameras!"

Jupiter said, "Why have you come to tell us this, sir?"

"The strange noises and 'ghosts' have been scaring the children and even the adults. A lot of people are now refusing to camp overnight on the Rock, as we usually do. It's spoiling all the fun of the week. If it goes on, the reunion may never be held again. And if Sam is the one doing the stealing, perhaps you boys can stop him before he goes too far or does something really foolish."

He looked at each of the boys in turn, and half smiled. "And I don't believe for a moment that story about a school paper, eh? I am well aware that Miss Hanson, your history teacher, assigned no such projects over the summer vacation."

The three boys squirmed a bit.

"I also have heard," the principal went on, "of your reputation as The Three Investigators. Chief Reynolds has spoken highly of your ability to solve cases that have baffled his men. I realized that you must be investigating Sam and that's why I came here."

"That's correct, sir," Jupiter told him. "Here's our card." He removed a business card from his shirt pocket and handed it to Mr Karl. It said:

THE THREE INVESTIGATORS
"We Investigate Anything"
? ? ?

First Investigator .... Jupiter Jones
Second Investigator .... Peter Crenshaw
Records and Research .... Bob Andrews

Mr Karl smiled and nodded. "I think you are just what I want. In fact, shall we say I'm hiring you to investigate the strange occurrences on Ragnarson Rock? Perhaps you should have a small retainer – to make everything official," he added solemnly.

"Wow!" Pete cried. "You mean real money?"

"Thank you, but there is no charge," Jupiter said. Pete and Bob glared at him. "Because of an unfortunate age requirement in the state law, we cannot be employed as licensed investigators," he admitted, "so we are happy to volunteer our services. Now I suggest we examine the new prints here in the workshop. Perhaps Mr Karl can see something we would miss."

Mr Karl helped them spread all forty-eight duplicate prints on Jupe's workbench. They pored over them but could not find anything that was obviously incriminating.

"How do we tell which one of those Vikings is Sam?"

Pete asked, puzzled. "I mean, they all look pretty much alike to me."

Mr Karl said, "He's the only one whose helmet has a nose guard. There, that's Sam."

There turned out to be sixteen photos with Sam Ragnarson in them. Most of them showed Sam clowning with the rest, battling the Chumash on the Rock, trooping back for food, making faces at Bob's camera, and generally playing the reunion game. Only two were different.

"They were taken one after the other," Bob remembered.

The two shots showed Sam alone behind all the others who were picnicking on the rise. In the first shot he was bent down over something they could not make out. The second showed him looking up, startled, his hand held out in front of him as if he were holding something.

"What's he doing?" Bob wondered.

"One thing he's doing for sure," Pete pointed out, "is seeing Bob aim the camera right at him."

"Yes," Jupiter agreed, "it's obvious he saw us taking the pictures at that moment. The question still is, what was he doing bent down like that behind everyone else?"

"Could he be hiding something?" Mr Karl suggested.

"Or burying what he stole?" Pete offered.

"Or picking something up?" Bob asked.

Jupiter nodded. "Any of those answers is possible. I think our next step should be to go out to the Rock ourselves. We can try to observe the 'ghosts' and noises, and perhaps we can discover why things are disappearing, and why our photos are so important to someone."

"That's no problem, Jupiter," Mr Karl said. "We'll all be out there later tonight, those who haven't been scared away already."

"But won't Sam spot us, Jupe?" Pete objected. "If he *is* causing all the trouble, and he sees us, he won't play any tricks tonight."

"I can fix that," Mr Karl said. "Most of us wear our Viking and Chumash costumes on the island, and we have quite a few friends out there who aren't known to everyone. I'll just get you costumes and tell everyone that you're friends of mine. You can have dinner with us and spend the night."

"Then it's settled," Jupiter said. "We'll tell our parents we'll be out on the Rock all night, pack our walkie-talkies, torches and sleeping bags, and meet you down at the dock – say in an hour."

"I'll have the costumes ready for you. Be prepared for a lively night!"

11

A Shape in the Fog

The motorboat coasted across the dark water of the small cove. An enormous bonfire and a bright moon lit the sandy beaches and the rocks. People moving around the big fire created fantastic shadows that seemed to flow and dance across the night. The edge of firelight reached out on to the water and guided Karl Ragnarson and the Three Investigators to the cove landing. The principal and Pete jumped out and ran the boat up on to the beach.

"Is that you, Karl?" the voice of Dr Ingmar Ragnarson boomed from the gathering above the beach.

"Yes, Ingmar. I have some guests with me."

"Good, good. Always room for more Vikings and Indians!" the dentist said. He wore a full Viking costume.

The boys and Mr Karl headed for the first circle of light around the fire. The school principal was dressed in the buckskin shirt, pants, beads, and dark war paint of a Chumash warrior. Bob and Pete wore the imitation fur tunics, helmets, and beards of Vikings. They carried shields and weapons – Bob, a long two-handed sword; and Pete, a battle-axe. Jupiter brought up the rear, dressed in the voluminous buckskin robe and painted wooden mask of a Chumash shaman. The First Investigator was not happy with his costume.

"I feel," he muttered grumpily, "like a walking mountain."

"They just didn't have a Viking costume that fit you, Jupe." Pete grinned. "Maybe if you'd lay off those chocolate-chip cookies . . ."

"You look very imposing, Jupiter," Mr Karl said. "A

shaman was the most important member of a Chumash expedition."

"You always wanted to be a magician, First," Bob added, hiding a grin as Jupiter clomped ponderously behind them in the oversize robe and grotesque mask.

"The magic I have in mind at the moment is to make you two comedians disappear," the overweight boy threatened. "You don't look so great in those moth-eaten bathrobes and tin pots either."

Bob and Pete looked at each other and burst out laughing. The two Ragnarsons laughed, too, and even Jupiter had to chuckle behind the mammoth wooden mask. They reached the enormous bonfire, where Dr Ragnarson introduced them as friends of Karl's who had come to swell the ranks of the celebrants. They were applauded by the fifteen or so people around the fire and immediately handed paper plates of barbecued ribs, corn on the cob, baked beans, and salad.

"Look for Sam," Bob whispered.

"And anything that might be at all suspicious in anyone's actions," Jupiter added, somehow managing to shove meat and beans through the gaping mouth opening of the wooden mask.

As they sat down in the circle around the fire, they quietly observed the people. They were in costume as Chumash or Vikings and were eating their dinners, which had been cooked over a great pit of coals next to the blazing fire. Rows of tents were up on a bluff above the beach at the edge of the wide circle of firelight.

"Anyone see Sam Ragnarson?" Pete whispered.

"Not yet," Bob said. "But I see the hardware store owner."

George Ragnarson sat on the far side of the fire in ordinary clothes, eating an enormous plate of food.

"The only one not in costume," Jupiter observed.

Everyone around the fire was friendly and talkative,

telling anecdotes and laughing. A few had guitars or accordions and someone soon began to sing. Then everyone was singing – old Scandinavian songs and American folk songs. The boys joined in whenever they knew the words, and when they didn't they hummed as loudly as the rest.

They were humming away with the happy crowd when Bob suddenly whispered, "There!"

Jupiter, Pete, and Mr Karl looked.

"Yes, that's Sam," the school principal whispered back.

"I wonder where he's been," Jupiter mused.

"He seemed to come from the direction of the tents," Bob said.

In the Viking costume he had worn the day he accosted the boys at the Rocky Beach dock, Sam had joined the circle around the blazing bonfire and seemed to be singing as hard as the rest. The music went on even after everyone had finished eating and had thrown their paper plates and plastic knives and forks into the rubbish bins set up around the beach. As the night grew colder and a patchy sea fog began to roll in, many of the people returned to the mainland, including George Ragnarson. The boys kept singing and watched Sam Ragnarson.

"All he's doing is eating and singing," Pete noted.

"He's certainly eating plenty," Bob replied.

"You could be wrong about Sam, boys," Mr Karl said. "Perhaps the trouble is all due to someone else, or something else."

"It could be someone else," Jupiter agreed. "But it would have to be someone on this island."

"What do you mean, or some . . . thing, Mr Karl?" Pete asked.

"I mean," Mr Karl said, "the noises and 'ghosts' could be some natural occurrence, tricks of light and sound, and the missing things could just be coincidences – a lot of

72

things lost at the same time due to all the confusion out here."

Jupiter shook his head in the gaudy wooden mask. "That would be an awful lot of coincidences. No, I'm convinced it is all one series of events, and we must find the connection and the reason behind it all."

"Jupe!" It was Pete. The Second Investigator was staring across the bonfire to the spot where Sam Ragnarson had been singing.

"He's gone!" Bob exclaimed.

There were only four other people in the circle now, and Sam wasn't one of them! Jupiter jumped up as fast as he could with the heavy wooden mask on, his bulky body staggering in the thick robe of the Chumash shaman.

"Hurry, fellows," he urged, his voice muffled by the mask which had slipped sideways on his head. "But first, someone straighten this ridiculous thing!"

A grinning Bob and Pete straightened the mask. Then the three boys left the circle of fire and plunged into the wisps of fog drifting across the moonlight. They hurried past the rows of tents and out across the treeless landscape of the mile-long island. They glimpsed the quick-moving figure of a Viking ahead of them in the thickening fog.

"It's him," Pete whispered. "That's the same costume he had on two days ago."

Indistinct in the fog, the shadowy figure led them toward the western end of the island, where the giant rock itself loomed ghostly in the moonlight like an enormous animal. There was nothing at that end of the island but the great rock, with thick brush covering its base.

"Where's he going?" Bob wondered.

"Wherever it is," Jupiter said grimly, "he's going fast and straight."

They moved on as quickly and carefully as they could behind the fog-shrouded figure, alert to duck for cover if he turned, but he never did. He just headed straight towards the large rock itself, and . . .

"He's gone!" Pete exclaimed.

Ahead, where a moment before Sam Ragnarson had been hurrying in his thick fake-fur robe and horned helmet, there was suddenly nothing but swirling fog!

12

The Ghost Ship

"He's just vanished!" Bob cried.

"That is not possible," Jupiter stated, staring around through the moonlight and drifting fog of the treeless island.

"Then where's he gone, First?" Pete wanted to know.

"He sure didn't climb that big rock," Bob observed.

"Maybe he flew over it," Pete suggested sarcastically.

"People do not fly, Second, and they do not vanish," Jupiter insisted. "There must be a place around here where he was able to hide, then run off when we couldn't see him."

Jupiter took off his heavy wooden mask and bent close to the ground. He moved in a small circle around the spot where Sam Ragnarson had vanished. The others followed suit, examining small areas on either side of Jupiter. The moonlight came and went, alternating with the fog.

It was Pete who found the tuft of fur. "Is this something, First?"

Pete was examining a thick evergreen bush about five feet tall. It was one of a row of juniper bushes that grew all around the eastern face of rock.

Jupiter reached below his robe and pulled out a tiny torch. He shone it at the bush. There were some broken branches around the tuft of fur, and behind the bush there was a space between it and the great rock – a space that led off to the left like a kind of natural tunnel!

"It certainly looks like part of a Viking costume," Jupiter mused, scrutinizing the imitation fur. "There's a piece of cloth attached. I'd say it had to have come off one of the Viking tunics. And Sam could easily have escaped from us by running along behind these bushes."

With Jupiter in the lead, the boys moved along the narrow concealed space between the thick juniper bushes and the steep face of the giant rock. The rock curved away to the south. Less than twenty yards from where they had found the tuft of fur, the bushes dwindled and the boys found themselves back in the open moonlight and drifting fog, the surf pounding close by.

"Gosh, that wasn't far," Pete noted.

"Far enough," Jupiter said grimly, "for him to run and come out here where we couldn't see him around the curve in the rock. That is how he 'vanished'."

"But where to?" Pete wondered, looking around.

They stood on a strip of rocky, gorse-covered moorland between the south side of the towering rock and low cliffs that dropped steeply down to the surf of the open sea. The treeless ground was cut by small ravines.

"There're a lot of gullies and depressions," Bob observed. "He could be hiding in any of them."

"But why, Jupe?" Pete repeated, his voice mystified. "He didn't seem to be carrying anything he could have stolen at the fire."

"That is the question, Second." Jupiter nodded. "And he's around here somewhere. How far can he get on this end of the island? We must spread out and search. Use your torches sparingly. We don't want him to see us."

"Jupe's right," Bob declared. "We've got him trapped."

They spread out like the police in the old Sherlock Holmes film who were searching the moor for the hound of the Baskervilles. The fog drifted across the island, growing thicker and then blowing thinner, the moonlight darkening and brightening. They searched the washes and gullies until the island ended in a tiny hidden cove on its westernmost edge, protected from the open Pacific by a spit of land to the south and a shoulder of the great rock itself to the north.

"We've lost him," Pete said.

"It certainly seems that way," Jupiter said unhappily.

He led his friends out on to the spit of land, but no one was hiding there.

"What do we do now, First?" Bob asked as he looked down at the deserted, fog-shrouded cove.

"Return to where Sam Ragnarson disappeared and see if we can find any clues we missed. And if we don't," the well-bundled First Investigator went on behind his grotesque mask, "we go back to the fire and see if the Ragnarsons have discovered anything."

With a last glance around the palely-lit landscape, they turned to retrace their steps – and froze.

Down on the shore at the head of the tiny cove, a shadowy figure crouched and shone a powerful torch out to sea!

Holding their breath, the three boys watched the torch beam sweep back and forth through the fog like a long finger searching for something. A sea wind had come up, blowing the fog thinner in patches, and then thicker again. The long beam of the torch continued to probe out beyond the mouth of the hidden cove.

"Jupe!" Bob pointed.

Out on the sea, caught in the beam of the powerful torch, a ship rolled on the dark night swells. Ghostly, it appeared and faded as the fog blew thin and then thick on the erratic wind. Tattered grey sails full of holes hung from its single mast. Grey shrouds seemed to cover the deck like a kind of fungus. The vessel loomed and faded in the beam of the light like a ghost ship.

"Wh-what is it?" Bob stammered.

"It's . . . it's . . ." Jupiter tried to decide.

And even as they watched, the ghostly ship with its

grey tattered sails and fungus-covered deck disappeared before their eyes. One moment it was there, rising pale on a wave, and then sinking back and gone!

The torch went out.

"Come on, fellows . . ." Pete started down through the rocks towards the shore of the cove.

The low sound like a growl reached them through the night. Then a menacing voice.

"Avast, ye knaves!"

The three boys started, and looked up.

The fog-swirled shape of Captain Coulter of *The Star of Panama* stood glaring at them from the headland above the cove. In his long blue coat with the brass buttons, his gold-braided cap and narrow trousers, he lifted his arm and pointed a skinny finger.

"Thieves! Trespassers!" he hissed.

A long, deadly cutlass appeared in his bony hand, and he advanced towards them through the drifting and blowing fog.

"R-run, fellows!" Pete cried.

Even Jupiter didn't need a second invitation.

13

Sam Reappears

The Three Investigators dashed off the narrow spit of land and made a wide swing around the Rock, trying to outrun their ghostly pursuer. In the mad race back to the safety of the camp fire at the other end of the island, Pete's helmet fell off and Jupiter lost his mask. Only Bob held on to his Viking helmet. As they neared the fire, Mr Karl and Dr Ingmar Ragnarson came to meet them, alarm on their faces.

"Boys!" the principal cried. "Where have you been? We've been looking for you everywhere!"

"What's happened?" Dr Ragnarson demanded.

"We . . . were . . . trailing . . . Sam," Pete panted.

"He slipped away," Jupiter puffed, trying to catch his breath, "while no one was looking . . . and – "

"Then we saw a ship!" Bob cried.

"And a g-ghost," Pete stammered.

"And somebody with a torch," Jupiter gasped.

Mr Karl held up his hand. "Easy, boys. Start from the beginning, when you left the camp fire."

"Well, sir," Jupiter said, still panting, "we saw that Sam had disappeared from the camp fire when we weren't looking, so we hurried after him and spotted him heading for the far end of the island and the big rock." The stout First Investigator puffed out the rest of the story of their adventure at the far end of the small island.

"The same thing again!" Mr Karl exclaimed.

"Except for the 'ghost' ship," Dr Ragnarson added.

"Yes," Mr Karl said. "Probably *The Flying Dutchman*."

"What's *The Flying Dutchman*?" Pete wondered.

"*The Flying Dutchman*," Jupiter intoned somewhat

pompously, "is a legend, Second. A sea captain who had done something bad was condemned to sail forever without ever stopping or reaching port until a woman would give her life for him. They even made an opera of the story."

"And a film," Bob put in. "I saw it a long time ago."

Pete gulped. "You mean it *is* a ghost ship?"

"Karl was being humorous, Pete," Dr Ragnarson said. "And instead of jokes and legends, perhaps we should go look at what the boys really saw, Karl."

"Take us there, boys," the principal requested.

"Second, Records," Jupiter said, "you lead the way."

"Sure," Pete said nervously. "Go ahead, Records!"

Bob glared at the other two boys but bravely started off.

The rising sea wind had blown most of the fog away by now, and in the moonlight they quickly reached the spot at the base of the giant rock where Sam Ragnarson had disappeared. Bob explained how they had found the tuft of fake fur and followed the hidden passage between the juniper bushes and the rock to the treeless moorland behind it.

"We were sure Sam had not come back past us towards the camp fire," Jupiter explained, "so we went ahead searching all these little ravines and washes, but we found nothing."

"Until we saw the torch in the cove," Bob said, "and the ship out at sea . . ."

"And the ghost of Captain Coulter practically on top of us!" Pete finished, shivering.

"All right, boys," Mr Karl told them. "Go ahead, just as you did before."

They moved through the clearing night, the wind sending the surf spray up over the low southern cliffs. When they reached the headland and the tiny hidden cove, they saw nothing moving in the dark night. With the fog gone, the sea beyond the mouth of the cove was clear, and there was no ship in sight.

"Not even running lights," Dr Ragnarson said as he shaded his eyes to peer out to sea. "There's no ship out there, boys."

They picked their way down the rocky slope to the narrow beach of the little cove. Jupiter glanced around.

"It was just about here," Jupiter decided. "Whoever we saw was crouched down and shining a big torch out to sea."

"Look at this!' Pete cried.

The Second Investigator bent down and picked up a large, six-battery torch.

Mr Karl examined the long torch. "That's the torch that disappeared from one of our tents, all right. Look, it's got Marcus Ragnarson's name on it."

"So someone did steal it!" Bob exclaimed.

"It seems like it," Jupiter said solemnly, "and whoever it was must have something to do with that ship out at sea."

"You think he was signalling, First?" Bob asked.

"Yes, or guiding the ship into the cove," Jupiter said.

"What about your ghost of the old sea captain, boys?" Dr Ragnarson said.

"We saw it back up there on the headland near the rock." Bob pointed. "We don't know if it had any connection to whoever was down here with the torch."

"Well, that ghost up there sure didn't want us around this cove," Pete said.

Jupiter nodded. "I think you're right about that, Second. Ghost or not, Captain Coulter did not want us to investigate the person with the torch. Since we first saw the mysterious captain in Sam Ragnarson's house, there would seem to be a connection between him and Sam."

"You think it was Sam down here with the light, Jupiter?" Mr Karl said.

"That is possible, sir."

"That would mean he had something to do with that ship you saw," Dr Ragnarson added uneasily. "Which could mean Sam is involved in smuggling, or worse."

"I'm afraid so, sir," Jupiter acknowledged.

"Do you have any suggestions?" Dr Ragnarson asked him.

Jupiter looked slowly around the tiny cove in the moonlight, and up at the headland in the now fogless night.

"The ghost scared us," the First Investigator said, "but I think we scared him, too. I don't believe anything else will happen here tonight. I suggest we continue to look for Sam, Dr Ragnarson. Perhaps he can tell us more."

Spread out in a line from the giant rock to the low cliffs of the south shore, they walked back slowly with their torches. They passed the great rock, emerged on to the centre of the island without finding anything, and continued on to the east end and the bonfire with the last few people around it.

"Look!" Bob exclaimed.

Sam Ragnarson, still in full Viking costume but with his helmet off now, sat calmly toasting marshmallows at the bonfire with two couples. When he saw the boys, he grinned broadly and waved mockingly for them to join him.

Pete and Jupe were still without the headgear they had dropped in their escape from the ghost.

"Well, if it isn't the Three Stooges," Sam said sarcastically. "I knew it was you guys as soon as you got out of the boat with Uncle Karl. Your fat friend here is a dead giveaway."

Jupiter was just opening his mouth to retort when Bob asked hotly, "What else do you know? Maybe you know who's going around dressed like Captain Coulter of *The Star of Panama*!"

"Captain who of what?" the sneering youth asked.

"You know who and what Captain Coulter is!" Pete insisted. "We saw him at your house! We even talked to him!"

Jupiter said, "You certainly know the captain and the ship your ancestor escaped from to reach this Rock. That's what this reunion is all about."

"I don't know what you're yapping about. I come out for a few beers with my cousins."

"Sam never was much for books and history, boys," Dr Ragnarson said dryly.

"But we *did* see the captain at Sam's house," Bob declared.

Sam scowled at the three boys. "What were you doing at my house anyway?"

"We went to ask about our stolen photos," Jupiter said. "You were the only one who wanted them."

"Tell me another," Sam said with a sneer.

"What about a man shining a torch out to sea at that little cove at the other end of the island?" Pete demanded.

"I've never been out to that end of the island."

"Where's your torch?" Bob said suddenly.

"Right here." Sam produced a large torch from under his fur robe. It was almost identical to the one they'd found in the cove.

"What do you know about a ship out on the ocean near the island a little while ago?" Jupiter asked.

"I didn't see any ships anywhere."

Dr Ragnarson watched his son in the light of the camp fire. The two couples left on the island had gone to their tents now. Only Sam, the boys, and the two older Ragnarsons were still at the fire.

"I think Sam is in the clear, boys," the dentist concluded. "There must be some other explanation for all that's been happening."

"I suppose so," Mr Karl said. "What do you say, boys?"

"It would appear that way, sir." Jupiter nodded.

"That's the first smart thing I ever heard one of those kids say,' Sam Ragnarson declared. He stood up. "I'm going to get some sleep, Dad. Unless I'm not supposed to do that either."

The youth slouched away towards the tents. Jupiter was thoughtful as he watched Sam go. Dr Ragnarson caught up with his son and began talking seriously in a low tone. Mr Karl watched them both until they disappeared in the dark outside the circle of firelight.

"What now, Jupiter?" the junior high school principal said.

"I suggest we all get some sleep," Jupiter decided. "The Three Investigators will keep watch during the night in case anything else occurs. Then in the morning we can search the cove and the other end of the island more thoroughly. Ghosts and people with torches just do not vanish into thin air."

"I'll watch with you," Mr Karl said. "In fact, I'll take the first watch, if you like."

"That will be fine, sir," Jupe agreed. "That means there are four of us, so two hours each should do it. We will keep our walkie-talkies on. You can borrow Bob's until he takes over the watch from you at one o'clock."

The Ragnarsons gave the boys the tent of one of the families that had refused to stay overnight with all the strange things going on. The Three Investigators discussed the events of the night for a long time without coming to any more conclusions. At last they settled down to sleep with the pounding of the surf in their ears.

Mr Karl stayed on watch until one o'clock, when Bob took his turn. The Records and Research man said goodnight to the school principal and then huddled next to the still-glowing coals of the bonfire. He stared into the red coals, listening to the wind and surf.

Suddenly a bloodcurdling howl pierced the night!

14

A Surprising Discovery

Bob sat frozen in front of the dying fire.

The howl came again. Wild and loud and terrifying, like the howl of a werewolf. Bob whispered urgently into his walkie-talkie.

"Jupe! Pete! Wake up!"

The howl came once more.

The howl of a werewolf!

Bob shivered and threw wood on the coals. His eyes searched the dark beyond the fire.

"Wh-what is it?"

Pete came up to the struggling new fire, huddled in a blanket against the night chill.

"I . . . don't know," Bob admitted.

Mr Karl appeared, pulling on his Chumash buckskin shirt, a rifle in his hand. He looked all around.

"It's the wolf howl we've heard the last two nights! Can you boys tell where it's coming from?"

As if the creature had heard the school principal, the howl echoed again above the wind and the surf. Bone-chilling, menacing.

Bob, Pete, and Mr Karl turned to look towards the giant rock at the west end of the little island.

"Somewhere down there!" Bob exclaimed, adding more wood to the fire that now blazed in the night. "It keeps coming from the same place."

"Yes!" Mr Karl said.

"Where we saw the ghost," Pete muttered.

Jupiter and Dr Ragnarson stood behind Pete and Mr Karl. The dentist wore a sweat suit for sleeping and also carried a rifle.

"The ghosts of sea captains don't howl like wolves, Second," the First Investigator said. "And I must point out that there are no wild wolves on this island or anywhere in southern California."

The menacing howl came again.

"Hearing is believing," Pete joked unconvincingly.

"It sounds as if it's near the big rock," Dr Ragnarson said.

Jupiter nodded. "It certainly seems to come from there."

"Are you sure there aren't any wolves on the Rock, Jupiter?" Dr Ragnarson said. "One lone survivor trapped out here?"

Jupiter shook his head. "No, sir. There never were any wolves in this region."

"Not real wolves," Pete put in. "But who says it's not another ghost, like Captain Coulter?"

"I'll agree on one thing, Second. I have a strong suspicion that whoever or whatever they are, the ghost and the wolf have the same cause." The First Investigator turned to Dr Ragnarson. "May I ask where your son is, sir?"

"Well," Dr Ragnarson said, "the last I saw him he was – "

"I'm right here, fatso."

In the bright firelight, Sam Ragnarson stood grinning behind his father. The only two Ragnarson couples who had not left earlier were now out of their tents. They shuddered when the bloodcurdling howl came again.

"I don't know about anyone else," one of the two women declared, "but I've had enough. Whatever that thing is, I don't want any part of it."

"Let's get off this island right now," her husband decided.

"I agree, let's pack up and go," the second wife said.

Jupiter held up a hand. "Listen, everyone, whoever's

86

making that howling is just trying to scare you off the Rock."

"Well, he's succeeded," one of the men answered. "We came out here for a little fun, not these terror tactics."

"If we all stay until morning," Jupiter urged, "I'm convinced nothing will happen, and tomorrow we'll find out what is making that sound, and what the ghost really is."

Sam said, "Well, I'm not going to wait. I say it's time to get off this rock."

Jupiter shot him a surprised look.

Mr Karl stood with Jupiter. "I suggest we all go and find out what's making that noise. Jupiter's right. There aren't any wolves on this island!"

"Unless someone brought one here," Sam suggested.

"Hold on a moment!" Jupiter said. "Think about the howling. It always comes from the same place! It doesn't move! A real wolf would move. A real wolf would be after food, would move towards this camp."

"Then maybe it's not a real wolf," Sam said. "Maybe it's something else."

"That does it," one of the wives stated. "We're getting out of here right now."

"All right," Mr Karl agreed. "The boys and I will go and investigate. At least wait until we return. Ingmar is armed. He'll stay with you until we get back."

"*If* you get back," Sam retorted.

The two couples said nothing. Mr Karl and the boys got their torches, and the four of them started out towards the giant rock once more. The wind blew hard across the narrow little island as they moved through the dark night, silent except for the pound of the surf against the rocks along the south shore.

They moved cautiously as the howls continued to pierce the night. Jupiter turned his torch on his watch from time to time.

"They come every two minutes," Jupiter observed. "It's too regular. No animal would howl at such evenly-spaced intervals."

They walked on across the treeless land, their torches probing.

The howl came again.

"It's that way!"

Bob pointed in the direction of the northern edge of the great rock.

Another howl rent the air.

"It-it's . . . closer," Pete said.

Mr Karl gripped his rifle.

The howl came once more – almost in front of them!

They froze, staring ahead into the night. They were at the northern edge of the great rock. Below them was a narrow open beach facing the mainland ten miles away.

The howl seemed to come from the beach. But they couldn't tell exactly where.

"Spread out," Jupiter urged. "It's the only way we'll pinpoint it."

Nervously, they separated and waited for the howl to recur. Two minutes passed. This time it was almost on top of them!

"There!" Mr Karl pointed.

"H-here!' Pete cried.

Pete was standing in the centre of the beach just below the face of the great rock. He bent down and picked up a miniature tape recorder.

"It's a tape," Jupiter exulted. "It plays every two minutes and echoes off the giant rock. There's your wolf, sir."

Mr Karl nodded. 'Sam has a tape recorder just like that."

"Many people have them," Jupiter pointed out. "It's not proof."

"Perhaps not, but it's enough to confront the boy with," the school principal said.

They hurried back along the length of the narrow little island. Dr Ragnarson sat alone at the fire.

"They're gone," the dentist said. "They wouldn't wait."

"A tape player, Ingmar!" Mr Karl cried. "No werewolf or even a normal wolf. A trick to scare people off the Rock, just as Jupiter suspected."

"But why, Karl? What could anyone possibly want on this godforsaken rock?"

"That is what we must find out," Jupiter observed, and looked around. "Where is Sam?"

"He went with the others," Dr Ragnarson said.

"He left?" Bob gaped. "Then maybe it's not Sam who wants us off the island after all! Maybe – "

"Fellows!" Pete shouted. "In the water!"

Where the glow of the fire just barely reached the water of the cove, three orange eyes seemed to stare at them!

15

Unwelcome Proof

"Wh-what *is* that?" Pete wailed.

The eyes seemed to move and then became long strips of glowing orange. It looked like a back, two arms!

"It's a person!" Mr Karl cried.

The school principal and Dr Ragnarson rushed to the beach and waded into the sea. The boys watched the two men bend over the pale figure in the water. Then they straightened up and came out of the water carrying a man's heavy canvas jacket.

"It's only a jacket," Pete said in relief. "With safety reflector strips on it"

"A jacket," Mr Karl agreed grimly, "but look at it."

The heavy jacket was torn and gashed all over – ripped and slashed. It hung in shreds with holes and dark stains everywhere. Mr Karl handed the jacket to Bob.

"Wow, what did that?" Bob wondered.

"Those stains look like blood," Pete declared. "I bet it was a shark. A big one too. It looks like a great white's teeth could have done this."

"You mean a shark got whoever was in that jacket?" Bob shuddered.

"I'm afraid so," Dr Ragnarson said.

Bob turned the jacket around in his hands and studied it. He unzipped a pocket and brought out a silvery object. "A cigarette lighter. With a car emblem on it: Jaguar."

"William Manning," Jupiter stated, "was a car dealer."

"Manning?" Dr Ragnarson said.

"A man whose boat we found." Pete gulped. "The police . . . haven't located him."

"It could be his jacket, Jupe," Bob agreed sadly.

"I recall Mrs Manning saying that her husband kept a two-way radio in his jacket pocket." Jupe felt in both pockets but found nothing else. "We'll show the jacket to the police tomorrow," he decided.

"Why not tonight, Jupe?" Bob said.

"There's no need to hurry, I'm afraid."

Mr Karl put in, "Anyway, the others took all the boats except mine, and with Ingmar here there are too many of us to risk a night crossing. We'd better stay until morning."

"And with Sam gone," Jupiter said, "I think we must remain for the night to be sure nothing else happens. I suggest we continue our guard watches with Pete and myself."

"The rest of us should get some sleep," Dr Ragnarson said with a yawn.

They returned to their tents. As Jupiter prepared to go back to the fire for his watch, Bob frowned.

"If Sam isn't making the weird noises, Jupe, who is?"

"Who else is on the island?" Pete wondered. "Except us and . . . and Mr Karl and Dr Ragnarson!"

"Yes," Jupiter said. "Only us and the two Ragnarsons."

The three boys looked at each other, and then Jupiter took his walkie-talkie and went out to the dying bonfire and the cold night. At 5 A.M. Pete shivered as he took over from Jupiter.

Pete woke Jupiter and Bob at seven o'clock.

"The fire's going good, and I'm starved," the Second Investigator said. "What's for breakfast?"

The two boys moaned and pulled the sleeping bags over their heads.

Then Bob remembered where they were and popped his head out again. "Hey, did anything else happen in the night, fellows?"

"Not a thing," Pete declared. "The way I like it."

"What happened," Jupiter mumbled from inside the

sleeping bag, "is that I froze to the bone, took two hours to thaw out, and got no sleep. Now go away and let me die."

"I thought you wanted to take that jacket to the police this morning," Bob prompted as he climbed out of his sleeping bag and put on his shoes.

"And maybe find out if Sam Ragnarson still has his tape recorder," Pete added.

With a muffled groan, Jupiter burst from the sleeping bag like a whale breaching from the sea. Once on his feet, he yawned, stretched, and rubbed his hands together.

"Right! But" – he grinned – "first we eat!"

"Now you're thinking straight," Pete said.

They hurried out of the tent and down to the blazing fire in the warming morning. A light fog had drifted across the island again, but the sun was rapidly burning it off as the day brightened. Mr Karl greeted them at the fire.

"Well, what will it be, boys? Sausages? Eggs? Hot dogs? Hot cocoa? Milk? Pancakes?"

They all voted for sausages, pancakes, and cocoa, and the school principal set out old blackened frying pans on metal racks over the glowing coals.

"Nothing more happened last night?" Mr Karl asked as he laid links of sausage into the smaller frying pan.

"No, sir," Pete said.

"Because Sam wasn't on the island," a new voice added.

Dr Ragnarson sounded unhappy as he squatted down glumly in front of the fire and warmed his hands.

"That is one explanation," Jupiter said, "but not the only possible one, sir. We were all on the island last night, and after we discovered the tape recorder trick, I doubt that anyone would try to scare us off again the same night."

"Nevertheless," the dentist said, "when Sam isn't on the island, nothing happens."

"Are you sure of that?" Jupiter asked quietly.

The two men thought for a moment.

"Well, I'm sure he was on the island whenever anyone saw the ghosts or heard the wolf," Mr Karl said.

"But things were found missing when he wasn't here," Dr Ragnarson realized.

"Which means nothing, because we don't know when they were stolen," Mr Karl said as he poured batter into the larger frying pan to make the pancakes.

Jupiter nodded, and they all sat in silence around the fire while Mr Karl cooked the pancakes.

"What do you plan to do next, boys?" the principal inquired.

"We will return to the mainland and continue our investigation of Sam's actions," Jupiter said. "Would you mind taking the jacket we found in the sea to the police? I want to inform Mrs Manning personally, and time is short. I need to re-examine those photographs as soon as possible."

"Of course," Mr Karl said. "It's tragic how people underestimate the danger of the sea."

Dr Ragnarson said, "What do you think Sam could be mixed up in, Jupiter?"

The First Investigator shook his head. "I don't know, sir, but I'm convinced he wants everyone off this island."

"Then why did he leave last night too?" Bob wondered.

"It also struck me as puzzling, Records, when he announced he was leaving," Jupiter acknowledged. "It could mean that something has changed."

Then the pancakes and sausages were ready, and they all ate hungrily after the long night on the Rock. All except Dr Ingmar Ragnarson who, worried about his son, only picked at his food. Then they doused the fire, washed up using sand and seawater, and climbed into Mr Karl's motorboat.

"We'll leave everything here," Mr Karl decided. "Perhaps people will come back when you find out what has been going on."

The morning fog had burned off and the day was bright and clear. The wind had died down, but the swells were high, and the heavily-laden boat chugged slowly towards the mainland. When they reached the harbour, Dr Ragnarson pointed to the public dock, where the motorboats were lined up.

"There's Sam's boat. At least he's not sneaking back out to the Rock."

The two Ragnarsons tied up the boat, and the boys retrieved their bikes from the harbour rack.

"What do we do now, Jupe?" Pete said.

"You and Bob go to Sam's house," Jupiter instructed. "Watch everything he does. If he leaves, follow him."

"What if he isn't there?" Bob wanted to know.

"Wait for him."

"What are you going to do, First?" Pete said.

"I will go to see Mrs Manning and join you at Sam's as soon as I can."

Bob and Pete went off to Sam Ragnarson's house while Jupiter looked up Mrs Manning's address in the telephone book. It was on the opposite side of town from Sam's beach cottage, up in the mountains. The hefty leader of the Investigators groaned inwardly – it would be a long, hard bike ride.

It was.

Puffing and panting, the overweight boy rode slowly up the narrow mountain canyon to the rambling ranch-style house set close against the foot of a dry, brown mountain. Around the large house itself, there was a green lawn and trees, the products of constant irrigation. Just as Jupiter rode gasping up the last slope, a man on a motorcycle came gliding silently out of the Mannings' steep driveway.

It was Sam!

16

Bob and Pete Find an Answer

Bob carefully scanned the beachfront street from the corner. Sam Ragnarson's dilapidated cottage sat silent in the sun. No one was walking along the deserted street.

"Let's get closer," Pete said.

They chained their bikes to a railing and slipped along the empty street to the cottage almost hidden by the dense jungle of untended plants.

"The garage is open!" Pete exclaimed.

Close to the side of the peeling house, they moved cautiously through the overgrown yard to the garage. One of the garage doors was ajar, and from the corner of the house they could see in. The brown pick-up was still there, but there was no motorcycle.

"It looks like he's off somewhere on the bike," Pete decided.

"Then we can search the cottage!" Bob cried. "And I'll bet we find Captain Coulter!"

"If there's a ghost in there, I don't want to know anything about it," Pete said. "I'll stay out here."

"No, not a ghost, Pete. A costume!" Bob answered. "I've got a hunch that it was Sam dressed up as the ghost."

Pete stared. "You mean that was Sam we ran into the first time we came here?"

"I'm almost sure of it, and I think Jupe is too," Bob said. "All we need is some evidence. If we search the house, maybe we can find it."

Pete looked dubious.

"Jupe said we should watch and wait for Sam to come back."

"But this is our chance to find out on our own what he's

doing," Bob urged. "Jupe can't always be telling us what to do. Detectives have to think on their feet."

"Well . . ." Pete hesitated. "I'll give it a shot."

"Come on, let's go around to the front."

Warily, they slipped back along the side of the peeling cottage to the sagging front porch. They climbed the steps softly and peered in through the dirty front windows, the ragged curtains open now inside. They saw no one. Nothing moved inside. Pete tested the window, but it was locked.

"Maybe a side window," Pete suggested. "Sam doesn't look like the type who remembers to lock all the windows."

"Why not the front door?" Bob asked, and turned the doorknob.

It was open!

Pete sighed. "That takes all the fun out of it," the Second Investigator complained.

Inside, the living room floor was littered with fast-food containers, soda cans, and dust. Dirty clothes were flung on the floor and over the broken and tattered furniture. The only drawers, in a table and a battered sideboard, were jammed open with junk.

The only thing they learned in the living room was that Sam Ragnarson was a slob.

The dining room was completely empty.

There were two bedrooms. One had nothing in it but piles of old car tyres, side and rearview mirrors, wheel covers, door handles, seat covers, and other assorted parts that could be sold. There were supermarket shopping trolleys, brass fittings for doors, and old doors themselves.

"I'll bet he steals this stuff and sells it," Pete said.

"That's possible, Second," Bob agreed. "But I don't see anything that tells us what he's doing on Wreckers' Rock."

The second bedroom had an unmade, crumpled bed that smelled as if it hadn't been changed in months, a single bureau, and a closet.

"Nothing here," Pete said from inside the closet.

The last room was the kitchen, where they had seen "Captain Coulter" on their last visit. The kitchen was dirty and cluttered, with almost empty shelves and a rancid refrigerator.

"That's it," Bob said, disappointed. "No clues anywhere."

"We still haven't searched the garage," Pete said.

"You're right!"

They hurried out to the tumbledown garage with its bare boards and gaps. Inside, Pete pointed to a patch of oil that showed where a motorcycle had stood. Bob nodded. Then they both saw the door at the rear.

"It looks like a storeroom," Bob guessed.

The door was closed but not locked. Inside was a small, narrow room cluttered with fishing gear, surfboards, bicycle parts, pieces of a skateboard, and even what looked like sections of a large hang glider. A small window lit the interior dimly. At the far end there was a workbench.

"There's Sam's Viking costume!" Pete cried.

The fur tunic hung on a nail on the wall. The helmet and leggings and leather wrappings were piled on the workbench. The shield, sword, and a small duffel bag were on the floor. Pete opened the bag. He looked up at Bob.

"Here're our ghosts, Records!"

In the duffel bag were the captain's peaked cap with gold braid, the long navy blue coat with the brass buttons, the narrow trousers, the old-fashioned boots, and the telescope. The cutlass wasn't there. There also shredded sailor's clothes and seaweed – the other "ghost" the Ragnarsons had seen.

"Bingo!" cried Pete.

"So Sam *is* the ghosts, just as I thought!" Bob crowed. "That was him in the costume the first time we came here!"

"He disguised his voice and acted real old," Pete said. "Anyway, we didn't know what Sam really looked like then!"

"No," Bob agreed. "We must have interrupted him when he was practicing his ghost act. He was trying out different poses and checking his reflection in the kitchen window."

"See what else we can find, Records."

Pete searched through the clutter that covered the floor of the small storage room while Bob examined the work-bench. Pete crawled around in the corners. Bob climbed up to the rafters. It was Bob who found the box hidden on top of a plank of wood. He jumped down and held it out open to Pete.

"What is it?"

"I think it's the whole story," Bob said. "The story of why Sam wants everyone off Wreckers' Rock."

Pete came and looked. Inside the box he saw five large coins. Shining gold coins. And some gold-coloured lumps. Bob picked up one of the coins.

"Dated 1847," Bob read. "And I bet those lumps are gold nuggets."

The two boys looked at each other.

"The missing gold from *The Star of Panama*!" Pete whistled softly under his breath.

"Sam found it on the Rock," Bob said.

"And he wants everyone off so he can look for the rest of it!" Pete realized.

The sudden roar of a motorcycle came out of nowhere. Frozen, the boys stared at each other.

17

A Puzzling Visitor

Outside Mrs Manning's house, Jupiter quickly turned his bike into the bushes at the side of the road as Sam Ragnarson coasted out of the driveway.

The motorcycle roared into life on the canyon road, and Sam raced past Jupiter without even seeing him. The sound of the motorcycle faded away and everything was silent again.

Jupiter got up slowly and pushed his bike up the steep driveway to the long, rambling ranch-style house.

He leaned the bike against the side of the house and knocked at the front door. A tall, serious-looking man in a dark suit and tie answered.

"May I speak with Mrs Manning, please?" Jupiter enquired.

"She's putting on some coffee in the kitchen. You can come in and wait with me."

The man sat in the living room and smiled sadly at Jupiter. He looked at his watch as if he'd been waiting a long time.

"Was the other man here to see Mrs Manning too?" Jupiter asked.

"Other man?"

"Sam Ragnarson. I just saw him leave."

"I didn't see anyone else here, son."

Jupiter sat and admired the expensive furniture and the modern paintings on the walls. The picture windows looked out on mountains all around. From the end of the long living room there was a panorama of the distant sea. On a table he saw a framed photograph of a short, stocky, middle-aged man standing in front of a large sign: MANNING MOTORS, JAGUAR AND TOYOTA.

"I'm sorry, Steven, but . . . Oh?"

Mrs Manning stood in the entrance to the big living room, drying her hands on her apron. The slender, red-haired woman wore a simple black dress now and looked wan and pale. Her tired blue eyes were on Jupiter.

"I know you, young man, don't I?"

"Yes, ma'am, from the dock. My friends and I found your husband's boat."

She stared at him woodenly as if not wanting to remember that day and the empty boat. Then she sighed sadly.

"Of course. You're . . .?"

"Jupiter Jones, ma'am."

"Yes." She nodded as if somehow his name were important. She turned to the solemn man. "This is one of the boys who found William's boat, Steven." She turned back to Jupiter. "Steven is my husband's brother. He's as grateful to you boys as I am. I never thanked you for bringing the boat in. If you hadn't, I might never have known what . . . happened to poor Bill."

Jupiter suddenly felt that he didn't want to tell Mrs Manning what they had found. He went on bravely. "Um, my friends and I were out at the Rock last night and discovered something that may have been your husband's."

Mrs Manning's eyes were riveted to the boy's face.

"It's a heavyweight canvas jacket," the First Investigator continued, "with reflector strips on the sleeves and a cigarette lighter with a Jaguar emblem in one of the pockets."

"That's Bill's!" Mrs Manning cried. "Can I see it?"

"I'm sorry," Jupiter said, "it's at the police station right now. I'm sure they will show it to you."

"Was it . . . OK?" the woman asked hesitantly. "I mean, was Bill's jacket in one piece?"

The chubby boy looked at his feet. "Actually, it was torn into shreds and covered with dark stains."

Mrs Manning's face clouded with pain. "What . . .?"

"Sharks," Steven Manning said grimly. "My God. I guess we know for sure now. At least it's settled."

Mrs Manning started to cry. She sat down on a long white couch and sobbed into a small handkerchief. Steven Manning walked to her and touched her arm.

"I'm sorry, Phyllis. I'll go to the police station, identify the jacket, and come back this evening. At least it should convince the insurance company that poor Bill's dead and make them pay his life insurance. Will you be all right?"

The sobbing woman nodded, her red hair bobbing in the morning sunlight of the large living room.

"It was good of Bill to leave you so well provided for with insurance," Steven Manning said. "We can be thankful for that."

The brother nodded to Jupiter and left. The First Investigator listened to his car start and drive off down the steep driveway.

"Er, Mrs Manning?" he said.

The slender widow continued to sob quietly into her handkerchief. Jupiter shifted his feet, coughed.

"Er, could I talk to you for a moment, Mrs Manning?"

The redheaded woman sighed aloud, then raised her head. She dried her eyes and gave Jupiter a small smile.

"I'm sorry, Jupiter. The news got me upset all over again. Still, life must go on, mustn't it? What was it you wanted to talk to me about?"

"When I was riding up, I saw a man come out of your driveway on a motorcycle. Can you tell me what he was doing here?"

"A man? On a motorcycle? I didn't hear any motorcycle." She shook her head. "I have no idea what you're talking about, Jupiter. I didn't see any man."

"His name is Sam Ragnarson," Jupiter went on. "Does that mean anything to you?"

She shook her head again. "Not a thing."

"Perhaps your husband knew him?" Jupiter pursued.

She frowned, dabbed at her eyes. "I don't think so. Bill never mentioned any Ragnarson."

"And you didn't talk to a man on a motorcycle just now?"

"No, I didn't even know he was here. What do you think he was doing? What did he want? Could he have come to talk to Steve?"

Jupiter shook his head. "No, ma'am. At least, your brother-in-law said he hadn't seen him."

"Then I have no idea what he could have been doing."

Jupiter left her sitting alone on the couch, staring at her hands. The First Investigator walked around the side of the house to get his bicycle.

Once out of sight of the living room, he carefully pushed his bike along the driveway towards the garage and the rear of the house. It was a huge garage that could hold at least three cars. He studied the ground as he walked. He found nothing until he reached the back steps.

The steps led up to the kitchen. In the dirt of a flower border beside the steps, he saw the unmistakable print of a motorcycle tyre! On the steps themselves, up near the kitchen door, there were flecks of earth like that in the flower bed. They were still moist.

Sam Ragnarson had been at the kitchen door, and Mrs Manning had been in the kitchen when Jupiter arrived. The only question was – had they both been at the kitchen door at the same time? And what had happened to the coffee it had taken Phyllis Manning so long to prepare?

Thinking hard, Jupiter didn't hear the two men until they were on top of him.

Two men in ski masks. One with the tattoo of a mermaid on his bare forearm! Jupiter tried to run, but they were too quick. They caught him, and a hard, dirty hand clamped over his mouth.

18

Strange Behaviour

Bob and Pete heard the motorcycle stop in front of the garage.

"The window!" Pete whispered.

They tested the single narrow window of the storeroom. It moved. Carefully, they eased it up. It squeaked loudly!

The boys held their breath.

Luckily, the motorcycle engine drowned it out. The motor stopped, but they heard no footsteps coming towards them. Moments later, both boys had squeezed through the window and were hidden in the jungle-like yard, where they could watch both the house and the garage.

"Good thing Jupe wasn't with us," Pete whispered from where they lay hidden. "He'd never have got through that window."

"Shhhhh," Bob warned, grinned, and pointed to the front of the garage.

Sam Ragnarson, barefoot and dressed in old cut-off jeans and a ragged T-shirt, had come out of the garage whistling merrily and now pushed his motorcycle inside. Then the busy youth pushed both garage doors wide open. Bob and Pete watched him climb into the brown pick-up truck, start it, and back out of the garage.

"He's leaving!" Pete whispered in dismay.

"We have to try and follow him!" Bob started to get up.

"Wait!" Pete held his friend's arm.

The truck stopped in the driveway. Sam jumped out, ran back to the garage, and opened the saddlebags on his motorcycle. He whistled to himself as he took a bottle out of the saddlebags and set it down next to the pick-up. Then he climbed up into the truck bed, pushed back a large tarpaulin, and jumped off again with an empty five-gallon plastic jug and a funnel.

From where they were hidden, Bob and Pete watched Sam open the bottle, put the funnel into the neck of the jug, and pour the contents of the bottle into the jug. Looking totally pleased with himself, he kicked the empty bottle into the bushes, capped the jug, and put it back under the tarpaulin. He seemed to think for a moment, then went into the garage again.

"He's going somewhere with that jug," Pete exclaimed in the bushes.

"And we have to follow him, but how?"

"One of us could try to get into the back of the truck," Pete suggested.

"Under that tarp!"

Pete chewed his lip. "But he could come back out anytime and catch us."

"One of us will have to watch while the other gets under the tarpaulin."

"That means only one of us can get on the truck."

"Someone's got to wait for Jupe anyway, or go and find him," Bob said.

"Shhhhhh!"

Sam came out of the garage again, grinning. This time he had the small wooden box where they had found the gold coins. He put the box in the cab and stood thinking once more. He seemed to nod to himself, and walked around the pick-up to the back door of the cottage. The door was locked. He felt in his pockets and found nothing. Muttering, he went on around to the front door.

"Now's our chance!" Pete exclaimed.

"I'll get under the tarp," Bob said. "I'm smaller."

Pete had to agree. "OK, I'll wait here a while for Jupe

and if he doesn't show up, I'll go find him. Hurry up. If I wave my arms, Sam's coming!"

Bob crawled out of the thick vegetation and ran to the rear of the old brown pick-up. Pete watched the front corner of the house. Bob climbed up into the truck, slipped quickly under the heavy tarp, and pulled it over him until he was completely hidden and the tarpaulin looked undisturbed.

Seconds later, Sam came out of the rear door and hurried to the pick-up. Chuckling, he climbed into the cab without even looking into the truck bed, backed out of the driveway, and drove away. Pete watched nervously until the pick-up turned the corner and was gone. He waited a bit for Jupiter. Then he got his bike, left Bob's bike still locked to the beach fence, and hurried off to a phone booth.

Jupiter might have finished early at Mrs Manning's and gone to Headquarters to get more of their equipment before joining Pete and Bob. They had their walkie-talkies, but Pete wished they had their emergency signals too, in case Bob got trapped or even caught. Maybe Jupe had had the same idea.

There was no answer at Headquarters. Pete looked up Mrs Manning's address in the telephone book.

The Second Investigator rode as fast as he could towards the mountains and the inland canyon where the Manning house was located. He soon left the town itself and reached the rising canyon road that curved deeper into the mountains. Standing on the pedals, he climbed the sharp curves and reached the steep driveway of the Manning house.

He looked all around for Jupiter's bike but saw nothing. Mrs Manning herself answered his knocks.

"Oh, you're another one of those boys!"

"Yes, ma'am," Pete admitted. "Is Jupiter here?"

"He was, yes. It was so kind of him to tell me personally

about poor Bill's . . . jacket. I owe you boys a great debt. Why, if it hadn't been – "

Pete broke in. "Isn't he here now?"

"Why, no . . . er – what is your name?"

"Pete," the Second Investigator said. "How long ago did Jupe leave?"

Mrs Manning looked towards a tall grandfather's clock in the entrance hall. "Why, an hour ago, at least. Is anything wrong?"

"I don't know, ma'am," Pete said uneasily. "Did he say anything about where he was going?"

"No, I'm afraid not."

"Did anything happen while he was here? Anything kind of strange or unusual"

"Not that I can think of."

Pete thanked her and went back to his bike at the side of the house. What had happened to Jupiter? He scrutinized the ground at the side of the big house, but found nothing except the print of a motorcycle tyre in a flower bed next to the back steps, but that didn't seem to mean anything. There was no sign of a bicycle tyre print.

Where was the First Investigator? Why hadn't he arrived at Sam's house as planned? It was unlike him to disappear with no warning. And it had been a full two hours since either Pete or Bob had seen him.

Worried, the Second Investigator pushed his bike slowly back down the steep driveway to the winding canyon road.

Then he saw the question mark.

It was on a telegraph pole on the right side of the road! A question mark scrawled hastily in white chalk.

Long before, The Three Investigators had devised this system of leaving a trail for others to follow when all other means of communication were blocked. The question mark was the symbol of The Three Investigators, and each Investigator used a different colour chalk. White was Jupe's colour.

Jupe had left the question mark on the telegraph pole!

Pete searched all around the pole. He saw the shallow tyre marks of a small truck and the narrow track of a bicycle!

The Trails Meet

Under the tarpaulin, Bob clung to the side of the truck as it careened around corners with its tyres screeching. Sam was blowing the horn and laughing maniacally in the cab. Whatever Sam Ragnarson was up to, he was very pleased with himself.

Once the truck stopped, and Sam got out to talk to someone. Bob raised the edge of the tarpaulin and tried to see, but whoever Sam was talking to was not in Bob's line of vision. All he could see was the building where Dr Ragnarson had his office!

Sam drove on once more, and when the jostling truck finally stopped again, Bob smelled the salt odour of the sea and heard the noises of the harbour. Then he heard Sam climb up on to the back of the truck. Sam was coming for the plastic jug under the tarpaulin right next to Bob!

The smallest of the Three Investigators made himself even smaller, shrinking as far away from the jug as he could without moving so much that he would give himself away. If only Sam didn't throw the tarpaulin all the way back!

Bob held his breath. A hand reached under the tarp, groped for the jug, and missed it!

Bob barely breathed.

The hand groped in again and found a small shovel by mistake!

Bob could hear Sam muttering and the shovel being thrown on to the pavement. Any second he might lift the tarpaulin to look for the jug! The groping hand came under once more. Taking a deep breath, Bob nudged the jug with his foot until it was an inch from Sam's searching hand. Then the last inch!

Sam grunted, grabbed the jug, pulled it out, and Bob felt Sam jump off the truck. He listened to the sound of Sam's footsteps going away on the concrete and then echoing hollowly on the wooden boards of some pier.

Cautiously, he peered out. He could see the buildings around the harbour and hear the traffic on the coast highway. He rolled out from under the tarpaulin and looked over the sides of the truck. On the pier where all the Ragnarson boats were tied up, Sam was bent down over Mr Karl's boat.

Bob quickly jumped over the tailgate and crouched down behind the rear wheel. On the pier, Sam had moved to another boat. He had the five-gallon plastic jug at his feet.

Bob looked around for better cover. An outdoor restaurant was just on the other side of the first pier. Bob walked quickly to the outdoor tables, sat down behind a potted palm tree, and watched Sam move from boat to boat on the pier.

Suddenly Sam jumped into his own boat, pushed it off, and started the motor. Bob stood up in dismay as Sam sailed away from the pier and down the harbour. Then he saw the boat turn and head for another large pier far down the harbour. Bob ran along the pedestrian walk towards the distant pier.

Pete biked down the winding canyon road towards Rocky Beach, searching the road and trees and bushes for any more signs of Jupiter. He reached a crossroad. Which way to go?

A round piece of orange-coloured cork lay in the road that led towards town. A question mark had been drawn on it in white chalk! Pete grinned. Jupe always found a way to leave a trail!

Pete scanned the road for any other signs. He found nothing more until he reached another crossroad. Once more there was a round piece of orange cork with a small white question mark to show which road to take.

Pete pedalled faster after that to the next fork in the road. He looked around for a piece of orange cork. There was none.

There was nothing at all with a white question mark on it!

Pete knew that Jupe would mark the trail when he could. Jupe must have been watched when the truck got to this fork. What Pete had to do was choose one fork and follow it until he found a sign or until it ended. If he found no sign, he would return and follow the other fork.

He took the right fork first, because so far the trail had always led towards downtown and the ocean. Less than half a mile farther along he saw a piece of wood lying almost in the middle of the road. A dark, worn piece of driftwood with a white question mark on it! Pete had chosen the correct fork.

The trail led Pete down to the harbour. The coast highway stretched straight ahead around the harbour itself with its handful of piers. Where was Jupe among all those piers and boats? For a moment Pete felt hopeless about what to do next. He thought hard. The orange pieces of cork were net floats – to keep a fishing net near the surface of the water. Maybe Jupe was in the truck of a fisherman who was going to his boat. So Pete's next move was to check the piers.

He biked slowly along the waterfront on the pedestrian walk that circled the harbour.

He spotted the tiny white chalk mark scrawled on another telegraph pole. The pole was at the spot where a driveway left the coast highway and entered the car park of a private commercial pier with buildings on it. Pete chained his bike to a bike rack above the harbour and walked into the car park.

The final chalk question mark was on the tyre of a battered white pick-up truck with a California licence plate beginning with 56. The truck of the men who had attacked Bob and his father to steal the photographs!

Pete looked around. The only hiding place was one of the buildings on the commercial pier itself.

He hurried across the car park to the pier and then looked carefully at each building. There were warehouses and storehouses for commercial fishermen, barrels and nets and rope piled everywhere. There were no other people around. By now it was afternoon and many of the harbour workers had left for the weekend. He searched the dirty windows for any sign of Jupiter. He studied the locked doors and the walls for a chalked question mark. There was nothing.

At the end of the pier, a single-masted trawler with nets hanging from its mast and boom was tied up next to the last building. Nets with orange cork floats!

Someone moved in the shadows between the high, two-storey walls of the last two buildings. Moved again, furtively.

Pete edged closer. The figure was crouched down as if hiding. It heard Pete and turned.

"Pete!"

"Bob?"

The two Investigators hurried to each other.

"What are you doing here?" Pete demanded in a whisper. "You're supposed to be watching Sam Ragnarson."

"I was. He came to this last building and was inside a while. Then he got back into his boat and sailed out of the harbour! I couldn't follow him," Bob explained. "What are you doing here? Where's Jupe?"

Pete told of his visit to Mrs Manning, Jupiter's disap-

112

pearance, and the trail of question marks. "I'm sure he's in trouble," concluded Pete. "Or else he would have made neat marks on every other telegraph pole."

Bob nodded. "He's got to be around here somewhere. But where?"

Both boys looked at the row of silent buildings at the edge of the harbour. It seemed as if the hefty First Investigator had evaporated!

20

Prisoner!

Jupiter glared at the two masked men in front of him. Tied to a straight chair in a tiny upstairs room with a single high window, he could hear waves slapping against piling somewhere beneath and smell the odours of fish and tar.

"I suggest you turn me loose before you find yourselves in severe trouble," the First Investigator threatened.

"He's got a big mouth," the taller one in the brown ski mask growled.

"Snoopy kids nosing around where they ain't wanted," said the shorter one with the mermaid tattoo on his forearm.

"I assure you, my partners will find me," Jupiter warned. "They will bring the police. Kidnapping is a very serious offence."

"A really big mouth, Walt," the tall one repeated.

"You want to see your friends again, kid," the tattooed one said, "you better tell us where all the prints of them pictures you took is."

"I'm afraid you're a day late," Jupiter replied maddeningly. "Mr Andrews printed the pictures yesterday in his newspaper."

"Would you get a load of Fatso, Ted?" Walt sneered. "We'll tell you when it's too late. Those pictures ain't the ones we're talkin' about here."

Ted stood over Jupiter threateningly. "We want all the leftover prints, tubby – now!"

"What are you and Sam Ragnarson doing on Wreckers' Rock?" Jupiter guessed. "What are you smuggling?"

"Who's Sam Ragnarson?"

"What makes you think we're doin' anything out on Wreckers' Rock?"

"We never go near the Rock."

"Too dangerous, right, Ted?"

"For sure."

"We saw you out there last night!" Jupiter ventured.

The two men in the ski masks watched him in the silence of the small room. The sound of the harbour waves against the piling below was loud.

"Sometimes kids can get too smart for their own good, you know what I'm saying, Ted?"

"A lot too smart," the taller one answered.

"They could be found floating in the harbour."

"If they was ever found at all."

In the chair, Jupiter gulped inwardly but kept his face expressionless.

"You can't intimidate me," he said calmly. "As long as you want the photos, you can't afford to harm me until you get them!"

"Don't be too sure, boy," Walt growled.

"There are three of you," Ted said. "If the other two find you face down in the harbour, your buddies might give us the photos a lot faster."

Jupiter paled but kept a grip on himself. Whatever the masked men were going to do to him, showing fear or panic would not help him. He made himself feel angry, even in a rage.

"What did we do, photograph your smuggling operation?" the First Investigator cried. "Is it gold? Illegal aliens? Drugs?"

"Smuggling?" repeated Ted. "The punk thinks we're smugglers."

"This guy's a walkin' brain," said Walt.

"Real smart," Ted agreed.

"If we're smugglers, we're real dangerous. Right, boy?"

said Walt. "You better just tell us where to find those photos."

"Just give us the prints," Ted offered, "and you go home all safe and sound. Every pound of you." He grinned sarcastically.

"Call your pals, tell them to get the prints over here," Walt threatened.

"Do it now, boy."

"While you still can."

"You want to go home, don't you?"

Jupiter swallowed, nodded. "All right. I'll call them."

"Now that's real smart," Ted said.

"And no tricks, kid," Walt told him. "We got your card outta your jacket and we know your phone number. Just play it straight."

Ted went out of the tiny room and returned with a telephone. He plugged it into a telephone point near Jupiter and, laboriously studying the Three Investigators business card, dialled Headquarters. Then he held the receiver up to Jupiter's head.

"Tell 'em you got an idea," Ted said. "You gotta look at all the prints right now down here to make sure you're right. Tell 'em to hurry."

"And do yourself a favour," Walt warned. "No tricks."

Jupiter nodded. It was possible either Pete or Bob had gone back to Headquarters to wait in case he called. If one of them was there, he would use a code message that would warn them he was a prisoner.

The telephone rang. And rang. There was no answer.

Ted slammed the receiver back in its cradle. "We'll wait, then try again."

There was a distant knocking on the downstairs door. The two masked thugs froze.

"You better take a look," Ted said.

The short one, Walt, went out of the room, reaching to

pull off his mask. Jupiter heard him go downstairs. There was a silence. Walt called up.

"Hey, Ted, it's the new manager of the fish market! Come on down."

"Be good," Ted warned Jupiter.

Jupiter heard the door of the small room lock. He strained at the ropes that bound his arms and legs to the chair. They seemed to stretch a little, but did not loosen. Desperately, he looked around the tiny room for anything that could help him break loose. There was nothing. The window was open a crack, but even if Jupiter hopped over there on the chair, it was too high for him to reach.

He was sure Pete and Bob had gone to look for him and discovered the trail of question marks. The first mark, on the telegraph pole near the Mannings' driveway, had been easy. Jupe had been facing the thugs with his back to the pole as they loaded his bike into the pick-up. With his hands behind him, Jupiter had scrawled the quick question mark. But after that it had been hard to leave a trail.

He had only been able to scrawl marks on the cork floats and single piece of driftwood and toss them out at moments when Walt, riding in the back of the pick-up with him, was looking ahead. The last mark had been the easiest, when they made him sit against the truck wheel while Ted checked to be sure no one was watching, and Walt watched for Ted's signal to take him to the building on the end of the pier.

With a little luck, Bob or Pete had followed the trail. But if he couldn't get loose, there was no way he could contact them. He strained once more against the cords that tied him to the chair. Then he sat back, breathing hard and feeling hopeless, his eyes still searching for anything that could help him.

He saw only his bicycle.

He stared at the saddlebags on his bike for some time.

Unless the masked abductors had taken it, his walkie-talkie was in there! He'd tucked it in there that morning after returning from Wreckers' Rock.

With a violent effort, the stout detective got to his feet with the chair still tied to him. His legs were tied too tightly to walk, but he could hop until he reached the bicycle. He dropped to his knees and felt one saddlebag with his nose.

The walkie-talkie was still there!

With his teeth, he pulled the buckle open, lifted the flap, and then, with his head propping up the flap, carefully pulled the walkie-talkie out in his mouth. It was loosening, slipping . . . Suddenly it hit the floor with a loud thud.

Jupiter held his breath.

He listened to the silence, the slapping of the waves against the pilings below, and the faint voices in between.

No one came.

He fell over on his side, nudged the walkie-talkie against a wall, and pushed the Talk button with his nose.

"Fellows!' he whined nasally. "Bob! Pete! Are you there? Come in, Second, Records . . ."

21

A Daring Rescue

"Bob! Pete! Are you there? Come in, Second, Records . . ."

Bob and Pete were crouched behind some crates next to the two-storey wooden building at the end of the pier. They had just watched a man knock on the building door and go inside. Now the familiar voice seemed to come up out of the pier itself.

"It's Jupe!" Pete cried.

"My walkie-talkie!" Bob exclaimed, reaching for his pocket. He quickly took out the tiny instrument Jupiter had made and pressed the Send button.

"First! Where are you? Are you all right?"

Jupiter's voice came out of the tiny instrument as if he were holding his nose. "Records? I'm in some building at the end of a commercial pier at the harbour. The same two who took your negatives abducted me from Mrs Manning's house. Where are you?"

"We're right outside!" Pete said eagerly into his walkie-talkie. "I followed your trail!"

"And I followed – " Bob began.

Jupiter's voice broke in. "You've got to get me out of here. I'm alone now, they're talking business with the fish market manager and should be busy for a while, but we have to hurry!"

Bob said, "Tell us exactly where you are, Jupe."

"I'm in a small room on what I think is the first floor of the last building on the pier. I'm tied to a chair. There's only one small window that's open about an inch, but it's too high for me to reach."

"What can you see through the window?"

"Nothing but sky, Records."

"What can you hear?"

"Waves hitting the piling. Maybe something heavy bumping the building."

Pete nodded to Bob and pointed to the fishing boat that bumped against the pier next to the building.

"Can you see anything at all out of the window, First?" Pete said into the walkie-talkie.

There was a silence. Then Jupiter's voice came low, "A small cloud, almost round."

Pete and Bob both saw the tiny cloud in the sky to the west. They hurried behind the building to the western edge of the pier, turned, and looked up. The single tiny window in the west wall of the building was high up, facing the water. There was only the smallest walking space between the building and the water on that side.

"OK, Jupe, I think we've got your window spotted," Pete reported. "What can you do to get out?"

"Nothing," Jupiter said from the walkie-talkie. "I'm tied to a chair, and I can't break the cords."

Bob and Pete crouched by the silent building, thinking. The trawler creaked against the pier. Boaters, water skiers, and windsurfers crisscrossed the open water of the harbour beyond the pier.

"Jupe can't get out," Pete said to Bob, "so we'll have to get up there."

Bob looked up at the tiny window one storey above them. "How?"

Pete considered. He walked slowly along behind the two-storey building and looked down at the deck of the trawler bobbing on the harbour waves.

"Hey! There's a rope on the deck! And I think we can pull the boom on the trawler around close to the window so that one of us can climb in!"

Bob looked up at the trawler boom and at the small

window. "Which one of us? As if I didn't know." He made a face.

"This is your lucky day!" Pete kidded him. "It'll have to be the smallest and lightest, Records. We don't know how much weight the rope or the boom can take, and Jupe'll be on the other end when you come down!"

The two boys jumped down on to the deck of the trawler, and Pete picked up an end of the long, coiled rope. He tied the rope around Bob's waist and explained his plan as he tied.

"You climb up the net to the end of the boom, and then I swing the boom around with the other rope until you're at the window. You climb inside, and I lower you down on your rope. You cut Jupe loose, and I'll haul you both up, one at a time. Then you grab the boom again, I swing it around, and you both come back down the net!"

Bob looked dubious. "I don't know, Second. It sounds like there's an awful lot to go wrong."

"The only thing that could go wrong is we get caught by those guys who grabbed Jupe, so let's hurry. Here's my pocketknife to set Jupe free. When you're ready to leave the warehouse, pull on the rope."

The rope tied, Bob started up the net. Climbing it was easier that he'd expected – the net acted like a ladder. When he reached the top of the long boom that angled out from the base of the single mast, Pete pulled on a second rope and swung the boom around until Bob could touch the window. The Records and Research man eased up the window and climbed on to the sill.

On the deck of the trawler, Pete braced and held the boom rope tight as he watched Bob lower himself over the sill inside. Then the Second Investigator eased Bob's climbing rope out and Bob disappeared inside.

In the room, Jupiter looked up from where he lay on his side and grinned as Bob came down from the window on the rope. As soon as the Records and Research man touched the floor, he untied his climbing rope and hurried to Jupiter.

"Hurry up!" said Jupe. "They'll be back any minute!"

A few quick cuts with Pete's pocketknife severed the ropes that bound Jupiter to the chair.

Bob and Jupe ran back to the window, carrying the chair. First Bob stood on the chair and hoisted himself up on to the high windowsill.

Jupiter came next. He stood on the chair, grabbed Bob's hand, and, puffing and grunting, finally made it on to the sill. Getting through the narrow window was a tight squeeze for the stocky First Investigator. He finally burst through like a cork coming out of a bottle and grabbed the net at the end of the boom. Once Bob and Jupe had good holds on the net, Pete hauled hard on the boom rope to swing the boom away from the window.

But he had underestimated the force of Jupiter's added weight. As the boom swung away from the window, the rope tore from his hand and the boom went right on swinging out over the water. It stopped with a jolt when it reached the end of its arc. Jupiter and Bob lost their grip, flailed through the air, and plunged with two great splashes into the harbour.

Both came up blowing like porpoises.

"Throw us a rope!" Jupiter gasped.

On the deck of the trawler, Pete was laughing like a hyena. There was an angry shout behind him. He whirled to see the two masked men heading for him.

"Swim for shore!" Pete cried. And he leaped into the harbour to join his friends.

All three boys swam for the harbour beach at the land end of the pier. They soon touched bottom and waded out, wet and bedraggled. First they blended in among the people on the beach, then joined the crowd of strollers on the walk.

"They won't follow us here," Pete said. "Not in those masks, anyway."

"Let's grab the bus and get out of here!" Jupiter urged.

"What about my bike?" Pete demanded.

"We'll retrieve all the bikes later," Jupiter decided.

On the bus the Three Investigators sat far in the back, their clothes still dripping. The boys got some surprised looks from the other passengers, but they were too involved in comparing notes to care. Bob and Pete told Jupiter what they had found in the small storeroom of Sam Ragnarson's garage and what Sam had done at the harbour.

"So Sam was the ghost of Captain Coulter, the ghost of the drowned sailor, and probably the wolf, too, and it's all because he found some of *The Star of Panama*'s gold out on Wreckers' Rock!" Bob finished.

"And those two in the ski masks must be his cohorts," Pete added.

"That's why he came to meet them!" Bob put in. "I bet one of them was out there on the ship last night, the other signalled from the shore with his torch, and Sam tried to scare us off dressed as Captain Coulter. The ship had come to carry the gold away!"

"Perhaps, Records," Jupiter mused, "but somehow I don't see why Sam would need them to help him get the gold."

"Then what else are they doing out there, and why did Sam go talk to them at the pier today?" Pete demanded.

"It looks like they're working together, all right," Jupiter admitted. "Sam must have spotted me up at Mrs Manning's house after all, and sent them back to abduct me."

"Sam was up at the Manning house?" Bob asked.

"Yes. He probably heard from his father that I was

going out to see Mrs Manning, and he beat me there on his motorcycle."

Pete was puzzled. "Why would he bother to go all the way out there?"

Jupiter shrugged. "Maybe he just wants to keep an eye on us all the time. Anyway, I asked Mrs Manning if she'd talked to him, but neither she nor her brother-in-law had seen him. I guess Sam was hiding somewhere outside. No, wait. His bike tyre showed in the dirt right by the kitchen door. I guess he wasn't hiding. So why didn't anyone see him . . .?"

The First Investigator stopped, confused.

"Something isn't adding up," he finally said. "Let's go back to Headquarters and think this case through!"

22

Sam's Game

In their hidden trailer headquarters, the three boys again spread the forty-eight duplicate prints across the desk and tables and file cabinet. Pete and Bob quickly located the ones with Sam Ragnarson in them.

"There he is," Pete said, pointing, "bending down behind the others. I'll bet he was finding those gold coins and nuggets."

"He saw me taking the pictures," Bob said, "and that's why he wanted to get them back."

Jupiter walked slowly around the room, studying the prints one by one as the Three Investigators reviewed the case.

"Yes, those must be the pictures Sam wanted," the leader of the team agreed. "They don't really show what he's doing, but he doesn't know that, and doesn't want to take a chance that the coins showed. He wants everyone off the Rock so he can look for more gold. That's why he played the tape of the wolf howls out there, and dressed up like a ghost."

Jupiter went on moving from print to print.

"And those two men in ski masks are working with him. They stole our negatives for him and tried to steal the duplicate prints," Bob summarized. "Sam sent them to kidnap you and went to talk to them to find out if they'd got the prints yet. He doesn't want anyone else to know he found the gold."

"Maybe he's already found all of it," Pete guessed. "He hid it on the island and the other two crooks are going to use that fishing boat to get it off and take it somewhere safe."

"That's what they were going to do last night in the fog," Bob realized, "but we scared them off. I'll bet they decided to try last night just because there was a fog, even though everyone wasn't off the Rock yet!"

"Yes." Jupiter nodded thoughtfully. "That is a logical explanation. But we're back to the same problem. Why did Sam need these two men? Why not keep the gold all for himself? He could hide it out on the island and bring it in a piece at a time as long as no one knew he had it."

"Maybe he needed them because he thought we'd spotted his game in the photos," Pete suggested. "He wanted to bring all the gold in fast."

"That's possible, Second," Jupiter agreed, frowning. "Still, I can't see how Sam could have sent them yesterday to attack Mr Andrews before even seeing the six photos in the newspaper. And remember, even Dr Ragnarson said Sam was out on the island when they grabbed the negatives from Bob on Wednesday."

"But if Sam didn't send those two guys for the photos, First," Bob wondered, "who did?"

"Besides," Pete pointed out, "Bob just saw Sam talk to them on the pier!"

"True," Jupiter admitted. "They must be working together."

"So shouldn't we tell Dr Ragnarson and Mr Karl?" Bob said. "And maybe the police?"

Jupiter pinched his lower lip – a sure sign of heavy thinking. He stared at the rows of photos. "We don't have any real proof that Sam has the gold, not without the coins. And I'm not sure that finding the gold is all that's going on out there. Also, the only crime that has been committed is the kidnapping, and we can't pin that on Sam without some evidence. No, I think we must catch Sam red-handed before we can go to the police. And the place to do that is Wreckers' Rock. We will go out to the Rock again tonight with Dr Ragnarson and Mr Karl. I suggest we go home to get our warm clothes and tell our parents we'll possibly be out there all night again."

They all crawled out through Tunnel Two, and Bob and Pete jogged off towards their houses. It was already after five o'clock when Bob arrived home. His father was in the living room.

"Anything more about those two men who tried to steal your photos, Bob?"

"We think they're working with Sam Ragnarson, Dad. He found the gold of *The Star of Panama* and doesn't want anyone to know it."

"And you took pictures of the gold!"

"That's what we think. Or something like that."

Bob hurried to his room for his jacket and came back down almost at once.

"Dad, tell Mum I won't be home for dinner. We're going out to Ragnarson Rock again. We might stay all night."

"All right, Bob."

In the warm evening sun Bob hurried back to the salvage yard, arriving just as Pete did. Jupiter was waiting for them. The First Investigator was excited.

"Hurry, fellows, Hans is already in the truck! We have to return to the harbour at once and go out to the Rock before it gets totally dark!"

"Gosh, Jupe," Pete exclaimed, "what's happened?"

"I'm not sure, Second," the leader of the team said quickly, "but I've been studying the photographs again, and if I'm right, there is something much more dangerous going on out on Wreckers' Rock than we imagined!"

"But why the hurry, First?" Bob asked as they trotted to where Hans was waiting with the salvage yard truck.

"Because Sam is already out there, and after dark may be too late."

"What about Dr Ragnarson and Mr Karl?" Bob wondered.

"They are already at the harbour," Jupiter said. "I called them after you left. They, and anyone else who is still willing to go out to the Rock, plan to leave the harbour at six o'clock."

"What about our costumes?" Pete asked.

"There's little point in them any more," Jupiter said thankfully. "Sam knows who we are and what we're doing."

They climbed into the back of the truck and Hans drove off towards the harbour. The rattling of the truck's ancient springs didn't allow for much conversation on the way, but Bob and Pete wondered to themselves what Jupiter had up his sleeve this time. They soon reached the Coast Highway and passed the pier where Jupiter had been held captive.

"My bike's still there," Pete observed gladly, and pointed to where he had left it locked to the bike rack.

"There're two bikes, Pete," Bob noted.

Pete saw the second bike next to his.

"It's Jupe's!" he exclaimed.

"Hans, let us out, please," Jupiter called. They parked and examined Jupiter's bike. It seemed undamaged and had simply been leaned against Pete's, saddlebags attached.

"Those two masked men were afraid I'd come back with the police!" Jupiter said. "So they brought my things out here and left them at the rack with yours. It's a good thing my bike wasn't stolen before we got here."

"How can we prove they kidnapped you now?" Bob wanted to know.

"We can't," Jupiter said grimly. "That's why they did it. With no evidence, the police might think I made it all up."

They loaded the bikes into the truck, and Hans drove on to the public pier where the Ragnarson boats were tied up. A few of the Ragnarsons were standing around the boats, waiting. Mr Karl and Dr Ragnarson came towards them.

"There's something wrong with all the boats!" the school principal exclaimed. "We can't get any of them started!"

"They've been sabotaged!" Dr Ragnarson said.

23

Back to the Rock

"That's what Sam was doing!" Bob cried, and told them about the five-gallon plastic jug and the chemical. "He must have poured something into the gas tanks that sabotaged the motors! He made it seem to onlookers as if he was just adding gas."

"Then he's out on the rock alone," Pete realized.

"Don't you have any other boats, sir?" Bob asked Mr Karl.

"Sam's disabled every one we've got!" the principal said angrily. "I just can't understand what my nephew is doing, or why."

"He was the ghost, and the wolf howl, and everything," Pete declared.

"Because he found the lost gold!" Bob explained.

"Gold?" Mr Karl said.

"Yes, sir," Jupiter told him. "When your ancestor Knut Ragnarson escaped the sinking *Star of Panama* and reached the Rock, the captain and his crew and the cargo of gold may have been there too – at least for a short time. We know now that at least some of the gold ended up on the Rock, perhaps all of it, and Sam found it when he went out there for this reunion. He didn't want to share it with any of you, so he's been trying to scare you all off the Rock."

"And last night he just about succeeded," Bob took up. "He scared off everyone except you two and us. Today he decided to sabotage your boats to keep *every*body off."

"Except maybe for those two fishermen," Pete said.

"We'll rent a boat!" Mr Karl declared.

"That won't be necessary," Jupiter said. "If my suspicions are correct, Sam is out there with two dangerous men who stole our negatives and kidnapped me." And Jupiter explained briefly about the two masked men, the attacks on the boys, and his kidnapping. "I fear Sam may be involved in more than finding the gold and he isn't aware those two are really thieves and kidnappers. Whatever Sam's done wrong, I think he may be in great danger, too. We must tell Chief Reynolds and have the police go out there with us immediately."

"Let's go and talk to the chief," Dr Ragnarson said.

"My car's closest," Mr Karl said.

The boys sent Hans home, and the five of them piled into the principal's car and drove quickly to police headquarters. Dr Ragnarson told the desk sergeant what they wanted, and Chief Reynolds himself came out to take them into his office. Jupiter explained the case briefly.

"I don't know how he got mixed up with those two men who attacked the boys and kidnapped Jupiter," Dr Ragnarson said, "but from what they've told us, Sam could be in real trouble this time, Chief. Let's get out there fast!"

The chief stood up. "I'm sorry to say it sure sounds that way, Ingmar. From the boys' description, those two are Ted and Walt Gruber, a pair of local fishermen who've been in trouble with the law before. The police launch will be waiting for us at the harbour. Let's go."

Mr Karl drove them back to the harbour, and Chief Reynolds soon arrived with three police officers. They all went aboard the police patrol boat, and the boat crew cast off at once. It was past seven o'clock and the sun was low on the horizon. Jupiter stood in the bow of the boat looking towards the distinctive outline of Wreckers' Rock.

"I only hope we're in time, Chief," the First Investigator mused.

"Why do you think Sam's in danger, Jupiter?" Dr Ragnarson asked.

"It's just a hunch, sir," the stocky leader of the trio said. "But if I'm correct, we must get out to the Rock as soon after dark as possible."

The chief looked at the sun. "It's going to be close, Jupiter. I'm afraid we won't quite make it before sunset."

"That will be just right," Jupiter stated. "It would be best if it's dark when we arrive, so we can go in unseen. But if it's been dark long, we might be too late. And when we do get close to the island, Chief, I suggest we cut our engines as far out as we can and go in without any lights."

"I'll tell the crew," Chief Reynolds agreed.

Chief Reynolds turned out to be right – the first darkness had settled over Wreckers' Rock as the patrol boat arrived. The boat's engines were cut to glide silently into the cove. The shadowy Ragnarson tents still covered the bluff above the beach.

The patrol boat had to anchor out in the middle of the dark cove, and the boys, the two Ragnarsons, the chief, and his officers rowed ashore in the lifeboat and two rubber rafts. They ran the boats silently up on the empty beach.

"Look," Pete whispered.

"It's Sam's boat," Dr Ragnarson acknowledged.

The small motorboat was drawn up on the beach, its outboard motor raised. It was the only boat in the cove.

"I don't see any other boats, Jupiter," Chief Reynolds said quietly, looking back out to sea.

"No, sir, not yet." The First Investigator looked around in the growing darkness of the Rock. "If I'm right about what Sam is doing with those two fishermen, I think we should look at the other.end of the island near the Rock itself."

"Very well, Jupiter," Chief Reynolds said. "I suggest we spread out to cover the whole island."

Chief Reynolds gave the orders to his officers. Bob was

on the north side and Mr Karl walked along the edge of the low southern bluffs. The rest were spread out in between, with the police spaced at intervals to come to the aid of anyone who might need help. They all advanced slowly along the tiny island towards the giant rock at the western end.

When they reached the juniper bushes at the rock's base, they all moved southward to cross the moorlike strip of land between the rock and the open sea. It was Pete who tripped over the small wooden box lying on the uneven ground. Gold coins and nuggets spilled out of it.

"Sam's got to be around here somewhere," the Second Investigator said softly. "Looks like he dropped his box."

But aside from the box, there was no sign of Sam Ragnarson.

"We'd better keep searching for him," Chief Reynolds said.

"I think, Chief," Jupiter suggested quietly, "I have a better way of finding him!"

24

Jupiter Exposes a Fraud

"What way, Jupiter?" Chief Reynolds asked.

"If you'll follow me, Chief," Jupiter said, "I believe I can show you. Everyone be quiet, and don't use your torches."

The First Investigator walked ahead on to the narrow spit of land above the tiny cove at the very end of the island. The others followed silently. There was no fog, but the moon wasn't up yet, and they all had to pick their way carefully.

"This is where we saw the g-ghost," Pete whispered.

"But there isn't any ghost," Bob reminded the Second Investigator. "It was Sam disguised as Captain Coulter."

"Keep telling me that," Pete said.

Jupiter put his finger to his lips and crouched down, studying the great rock that loomed over the far side of the cove, the headland at the rear of the cove, and the cove itself.

"What are you watching for, Jupiter?" Chief Reynolds whispered.

"Well, sir," Jupiter began softly. "I think – "

From somewhere down on the shore of the tiny cove, a light began to blink on and off, its beam aimed out to sea.

"Is that Sam?" Chief Reynolds whispered.

Before Jupiter could answer, Pete's hoarse whisper came, almost too loud. "Fellows! Look!"

The running lights of a ship had appeared out on the sea and were moving swiftly in towards the island. The ship glided in through the mouth of the cove and dropped anchor. A bright light on its wheelhouse illuminated the whole cove.

"It's the ghost ship!" Bob cried quietly.

It was the single-masted ship with the "torn" grey sails they had seen in the fog. Now they could see that the "sails" were the nets hanging from the long boom, and the "ghost ship" was the same trawler that had been tied up next to the building where Jupiter had been held prisoner. There were two men on the boat.

"It's the Gruber brothers, all right," Chief Reynolds said. "Are you sure they are the two who kidnapped you, Jupiter?"

"They look like them," Jupiter decided. "One tall, one short and heavy, but they had masks on each time we saw them."

As they all watched from the spit of land, the pair lowered a rubber boat over the side of the fishing boat. The taller man climbed in and paddled to shore. He jumped out and ran the rubber boat up on the beach of the tiny cove, then stood there as if waiting for something.

"What's he waiting for?" Mr Karl wondered.

"Probably Sam," Dr Ragnarson said sadly.

Jupiter said nothing, only held his finger to his lips.

The solitary fisherman on the beach looked at his watch.

Jupiter turned to face the rock. "There," he said softly, a note of triumph in his voice. The others turned around.

Two men had appeared as if from out of the base of the great rock itself.

One was Sam Ragnarson.

The other was a short, stocky, middle-aged man wearing light pants and a ski jacket.

"The jacket!" Mr Karl whispered. "It looks like the one that disappeared from our tents!"

The stocky man seemed to push Sam ahead of him down the slope and across the small beach of the cove to where the taller fisherman waited at the rubber boat. Sam stumbled and dragged his feet as if he didn't want to go to the rubber boat. Something glinted in the hand of the stocky man.

"It's a knife," Dr Ragnarson said in alarm. "He's holding Sam prisoner!"

Chief Reynolds stood up. "Halt! Police! You are all under arrest! Drop that knife and freeze!"

The police shone their torches and pointed their guns at the stocky man, Sam, and the tall man at the raft. One of the police officers had gone out to the end of the spit and had a gun and light trained on the short man on the trawler.

"His arm!" Pete cried. "On the short guy. It's got a mermaid tattoo!"

"Then it *was* the Gruber brothers who grabbed me," Jupiter stated grimly.

For a long moment the man with the knife and the two fishermen seemed blinded as the police torches shone directly into their eyes. Then the stocky man on the beach dropped his knife and raised his hands.

Everyone went down to the beach – except the policeman at the mouth of the tiny harbour – and Sam wiped his brow. He nodded sheepishly to his father and the Three Investigators.

"I never expected to be so glad to see you kids," the youth admitted. "How did you figure it out?"

"Yes, Jupiter," Chief Reynolds wanted to know. "What's going on here? Who is this man?"

The chief pointed to the stocky man in the light pants and stolen jacket, who stood glaring at Jupiter.

"Meet Mr William Manning, Chief," Jupiter said. "The report of his tragic death was a trifle premature!"

"Manning?" Chief Reynolds stared.

"Yes, sir," said Jupe. "The man who supposedly drowned. It was just a simple insurance fraud scheme, I'm afraid. He planned to 'die' in a boating 'accident', then hide out on the Rock. His fisherman friends would pick him up and help him get out of the country. His 'widow' would collect his life insurance – I expect you'll find out he was insured for a large sum – and eventually meet him in whatever country he was hiding."

William Manning swore at the hefty leader of the Three Investigators. Jupiter went on unperturbed.

"Unfortunately, the Ragnarsons descended on the Rock right after Mr Manning arrived. He couldn't risk being picked up. Not until last night when most of the Ragnarsons had left the island and there was a heavy fog. He thought the fog would cover him, but we spoiled that."

"You can't prove any of that, you young punk!' cried William Manning. "I had an accident and lost my memory. I just woke up!"

Jupiter laughed. "Any kid in my school could come up with a better story than that!"

The car dealer scowled.

"You have quite a good deal of explaining to do, Mr Manning," said Chief Reynolds.

"He had quite a good scheme, actually," said Jupiter. "I think it would have succeeded except for the Ragnarsons."

"And the Three Investigators!" Chief Reynolds added with a smile.

25

A Visit to Mr Sebastian

"When did you first suspect that William Manning might not have gone to a watery grave, Jupiter?" Hector Sebastian asked.

It was a week later and the Three Investigators were settled comfortably in the deep leather armchairs that were the most recent addition to Mr Sebastian's enormous living room. The thin, grey-haired former private detective had just finished reading Bob's notes on the Mystery of Wreckers' Rock. He was wrapping up the case with the boys at his home in the Malibu hills – a former restaurant with a breathtaking view of the ocean that he was slowly turning into a comfortable retreat. A few miles up the coast from Rocky Beach, it was where Mr Sebastian wrote the novels and screenplays that were making him famous.

"Actually, not until I saw Sam Ragnarson at Mrs Manning's house, and she claimed not to have seen him," Jupiter declared. "That was hard to believe when I thought about it. But even before then, I wondered if someone besides Sam wanted our photographs. When Mr Andrews was attacked, there hadn't been time for Sam to view the pictures in the afternoon paper and then summon the two masked men.

"I began thinking that Sam's wanting to conceal the existence of the gold couldn't explain all the interest in the photos. So when Bob and Pete left Headquarters to get clothes for our second night on the Rock, I studied all the pictures again." He took four photographs from a manila envelope and laid them in front of Mr Sebastian. "If you look carefully, you can see a face at the base of the great rock as the Ragnarsons march down after the battle."

Mr Sebastian peered closely, then took out a magnifying glass and studied the pictures further. "It's not obvious unless you look very carefully, but there's a very surprised face peering out from behind a bush!"

"Right," Jupiter said. "It suddenly struck me – what if Mr Manning were alive out on the Rock? What if he had seen Bob take his photograph? And what if he couldn't afford to have anyone – such as a life insurance company – see those photos and know that he was alive? That would explain a lot of things that had happened."

Pete groaned. "I still don't understand what life insurance is all about."

"It's protection for a person's family in case he or she dies," explained Mr Sebastian. "You pay a small amount every month for the insurance. Then if you die young, the insurance company will pay a big sum to your family – a lot more money than you've paid in. They pay whatever you've arranged for."

"For Mr Manning, it was $500,000," Bob put in.

"Wow!" exclaimed Pete. "It's sort of like gambling, isn't it? Except you have to die to win."

"That's a crude way of putting it," said Mr Sebastian, "but yes, you could say both sides are gambling. The insurance company is betting that you won't die young, because very few people do, and that you'll keep paying them month after month. You're making sure that if you do die young, your family won't be left penniless. Mr Manning wanted his money without dying first. I assume he was in some sort of financial difficulties?"

"Yes," replied Jupe. "He and Mrs Manning were big spenders, but car sales had really slacked off in the last few years. And their scheme seemed so simple. Fake the accident with a little blood on the boat and his hat, and toss a ripped and bloodied jacket overboard. Then hide on the Rock until night, when the Grubers would pick him up."

"But the Ragnarsons' reunion and Bob's photos ruined it," Pete finished, grinning.

"Manning saw Bob take the photos," said Jupe, "so he called the Gruber brothers on their fishing boat with his two-way radio and told them they had to get the photographs from us. And also that he couldn't leave the Rock with the Ragnarsons there. He hadn't planned to camp there, so he had to start stealing food and clothing from the reunion to survive."

"Why did it take the Grubers so long to rescue him?" asked Mr Sebastian.

"It was clear and bright the first two nights," Pete answered, "and they didn't want to risk having the Ragnarsons see them."

"But on the third night," Bob went on, "it was foggy and most of the Ragnarsons had been scared away by Sam. So Mr Manning took a risk and signalled his friends with a torch. It was a mistake. We saw him, and so did Sam."

"Ah, yes, that brings us to Sam," said the mystery writer. "Was he part of the insurance fraud?"

"No, he wasn't," said Jupiter, "at least, not exactly. At the start he just wanted to scare everyone away from the Rock so he could dig for gold in private. So he dressed up as a ghost and played that wolf tape. But then he saw William Manning on the Rock and realized who he was. Sam decided there was more money in blackmail than in gold. He went back to the mainland and called on Mrs Manning just before I did. Mrs Manning was forced to give in to his demands, and he started working with the Grubers to make sure Mr Manning could be picked up unseen from the Rock. That's why he sabotaged the other Ragnarson boats. Then he returned to the Rock with the Grubers."

"A foolish move for that greedy young man," commented Mr Sebastian.

"It sure was!" exclaimed Pete. "Because Manning and those guys didn't need a leech like Sam around. They were taking him off the island by force, and I bet anything they were going to feed him to the sharks!"

"No wonder he was so grateful to see you arrive," said Mr Sebastian. "And where is the barefoot gold digger now?"

Jupiter grinned. "Stuck at home. The judge put him on probation for aiding the Mannings and forbade him to go out to Wreckers' Rock."

"All the other Ragnarsons have been out there digging for days," Pete added, laughing. "And he won't get anything they find. He must be really mad."

"Not that they've found much gold," Bob put in. "A few more coins, that's all."

"So Captain Coulter and his murderous crew really did stop on the island and leave some gold," Mr Sebastian concluded. "But their fate, and that of the rest of the gold, is still the secret of Wreckers' Rock."

The Three Investigators nodded.

"And the Mannings and the Grubers – what is their fate?"

"Just what you've seen in the newspapers," said Jupe. "They were all arrested on various charges of fraud, assault, conspiracy, even kidnapping. They're going to be busy with their lawyers for a very long time. The only person who isn't in big trouble in that group is Mr Manning's brother. He didn't know anything about the scheme and really thought William Manning was dead. He's even madder at the Mannings than the insurance company is."

"So once again the good guys win," the mystery writer said. Then he went on with a twinkle in his eye, "How did Karl Ragnarson reward you three for successfully solving the case? I recall you nobly declined his offer of payment, Jupiter."

The First Investigator turned a bright shade of pink. "Yes, sir, you remember correctly. Uh, actually, Mr Karl was very pleased with the outcome of the case. His brother's mind was relieved, the reunion could continue undisturbed, and his nephew Sam came through unharmed."

"Then what's the problem, Jupe?" Mr Sebastian asked.

"Mr Karl thought it fitting that we accept a token of his appreciation, since we're unable to accept money." Jupiter dug around in the knapsack sitting next to his chair while Bob and Pete exchanged mirthful glances.

"And here it is." Jupiter pulled out of his bag none other than the Chumash shaman's mask that had been part of his costume on the rock – the heavy wooden mask that had irritated him at every step.

Pete and Bob collapsed with laughter. Even Mr Sebastian had to hide a grin with his hand.

"I'm sorry Don isn't here to see it," Mr Sebastian said. He was referring to Hoang Van Don, his Vietnamese houseman and cook.

"Yes, where is Don today?" asked Bob.

Mr Sebastian looked like the cat who swallowed the canary. "Don had to leave for a few hours for something amazing, which you will soon see. He prepared a sumptuous French picnic for us before he left, but he made me promise not to start eating till two o'clock, which is in five minutes. Follow me – it's time to eat."

They all went out into the kitchen and soon returned laden with baskets containing long French breads, cheese, homemade pâtés, and exotic cakes. Pete could barely restrain himself, and Jupiter's eyes glowed at the sight of the pastries.

"Eat up, boys," Mr Sebastian urged them, "and now for the main event."

The mystery writer turned on the television set while the boys reached for the food. The TV screen lit up and there, standing next to a jolly man in a chef's hat and apron, was Hoang Van Don, smiling broadly.

"Don wrote to the Gourmet Guru and told him how much he admired him, and this is the result," Mr Sebastian informed the boys. "This is Don's moment."

As they ate and watched, Don worked as the TV chef's assistant for the entire half hour, slicing and chopping and stirring. At the end of the programme, the boys applauded with the audience. On screen, the rotund and beaming chef also applauded Don.

"There you have him – Hoang Van Don, who has been cooking for only a year. Why, in a few years, he will be serving banquets to the famous."

Don beamed. "Already serve the famous. My boss, Mr Hector Sebastian."

Mr Sebastian looked gratified.

"The mystery writer, of course," the chef said.

"Also the Three Investigators!" Don announced happily.

Jupiter froze – an éclair midway to his mouth – and stared at the screen. Bob and Pete gaped.

"Ah, yes," the chef concurred, "the three intrepid boys who foiled the big insurance fraud in Rocky Beach last week."

"Ve-rry famous detectives! Jupiter Jones, Bob Andrews, and Peter Crenshaw. I proud to cook for them."

Jupiter, Bob, and Pete stared at the screen where their names were being announced to the TV millions across the entire nation!

"Now you really are famous, boys," Mr Sebastian said with a smile.

The Three Investigators gulped, then grinned from ear to ear.